siege duet book one

twisted
heartbreak

bestselling author
n. isabelle blanco

Twisted Heartbreak
Siege Series #1

Copyright © N. Isabelle Blanco

This book is a work of fiction. Names, characters, places, and incidents either are products of the author's imagination or are used fictitiously. Any resemblance to actual events or locales or persons, living or dead, is entirely coincidental.

This work is copyrighted. All rights are reserved. Apart from any use as permitted under the Copyright Act 1968, no part may be reproduced, copied, scanned, stored in a retrieval system, recorded or transmitted, in any form or by any means, without prior written permission of the author.

Cover design by Pretty in Ink Creations
Formatting by Midnight Designs

Publication Date: March 10th 2022
Genre: FICTION/Romance/Suspense
Copyright © 2022 N. Isabelle Blanco

All rights reserved

Life separated us.
Destiny tied me to her.
Obsession drove me mad.
I knew they all hurt her. What I didn't understand is how deep . . .

Seven years ago, they ripped her from me—my father. The friends I made at school. Jealousy drove all of those bastards into conspiring against us.

And they won.

I almost killed myself after losing her.

Now I live for only three things:

I will destroy everyone who hurt her.
I will find her.
I'll become the biggest monster ever known to accomplish those things.

I'm at the head of my father's empire now. A corporate king. I'm ready to finally put in place the plan I've been working on for years.

I'm ready to find my Lexi.

What I didn't realize is that she had already found me.

ALSO BY
N. ISABELLE BLANCO

Ryze Series
(Dark Paranormal Romance)
Lust
Silence
Vengeance
Cursed
Hunt
Sacrifice
Light (Coming Soon)

Allure Series
(Contemporary Romance)
To Want You
To Have You
To Lose You

Retaliations Series
(Romantic Suspense)
A Debt Repaid
Damage Owed (Coming Soon)

Siege Series
(Dark Romantic Suspense)
Twisted Heartbreak
Twisted Rage

Need Series (Co-written w/ K.I. Lynn)
(New Adult Angst)
Need
Take
Own

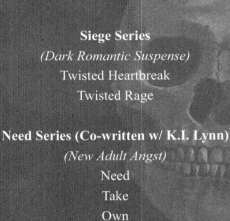

chapter 1

andrew

present

the wealthy don't have time to grieve.

It's a lesson my father drilled into my head over and over throughout my life. When my dog died. Again when my grandma died—both of them.

Yeah, he didn't let me grieve the death of his own mother.

If he mourned her, I have no clue. No one does. We never saw any sign. He just went about his business as usual.

He was a strict authoritarian, that one. Among other things.

I wonder if all those years he was busy drilling the lesson into my head, he'd known it would one day apply to his own death.

Food for thought, huh?

Well, in case there is such a thing as an afterlife, I want you to know, Old Man, that I learned the lesson very well.

I'm sitting here, at the top floor of the skyscraper you built, in what was once your office—an office that recently got remodeled to better fit my tastes.

And I'm calm. Cool. Collected. So unperturbed by your passing, Father—despite the fact that I caused it—that I'm starting to think something's wrong with me.

Then again, considering the type of man my father was, maybe all of this is perfectly normal. I'm not the only one that isn't aching over his passing. No one seems too broken up about it.

My mother isn't. I don't blame her. She put up with enough crap from that man.

His own brother isn't too sad, either.

So, like I said, maybe I'm normal after all.

"Drew. Are you ready?"

Speak of the Devil.

My uncle Richard stands at the entrance to my office, hand braced on the glass door.

He's been asking me that question ever since we agreed that I would be taking over my father's place as CEO.

My uncle refused the position and I had no choice. There are many on the board that would love to drive the whole Drevlow family right out of the company now that my father is gone.

I can't allow that to happen. Can't do that to my mother. She deserves all the comfort and privileges this company affords her. She went through enough being married to my father. I'm not letting her suffer anymore unnecessary bullshit.

And it was the perfect revenge against my father; the best way to get back at him for what he once did to Lexi's family.

"I'm going to take your place as CEO."

"It's about damn time you smartened up and decided to do the

right thing."

So much contempt. Even as he lies in a hospital bed, machines struggling to keep him alive, his feeble heart replaced with a new heart that his body is rejecting. Smiling coldly at the man before me, I lean toward him and whisper, "I'm only taking the position so that one day, when I find Lexi, I can give it to her."

My father's eyes bulge out of his head and his face turns bright red.

"That's right." I nod. "Once I find her, I'm going to make sure a Berkman *ends up in charge of your company.*"

I killed my father with that promise. Didn't lay a single finger on him. The last word left my mouth and the rage he felt exploded inside him, his blood pressure skyrocketing and sending him into yet another cardiac arrest.

I killed my father because he believed the conviction in my voice. He knew I was serious. That I meant every word.

It's that conviction that brought me to this point—the head of a company I didn't want to run, my feet on a black marble floor, surrounded by glass, steel, and gold accents.

Sitting behind a brand new desk, in a way too-big office, and metaphorically in the shoes of a man I came to loathe throughout my life.

For my mother.

And Lexi.

Wherever she is.

The power this company gives me will be enough to help me find her.

I *will* find her.

I can't even think her name without that old, crippling rage squirming inside me.

As I've been forced to do for seven years, I push the memory of her back. Remembering that I lost her, *how* it all came to pass, is toxic in ways my relationship with my father never was.

Until I can find her, I can't afford to wallow in her.

God I want to. Get lost in the vision. Let the ache consume me. It would be so much easier than this constant battle, always having to fight my own psyche and the way it yearns for her.

I tried that once. Almost lost my fucking mind. The pit I ended up falling into was too deep, darker than anything my human mind could've ever imagined. My self-destruction came close to spilling over into the lives of the few people I loved.

Because I loved her more than I've ever loved anyone.

More than I loved my own mother.

I still feel that way. Time has done nothing but make the emotions more powerful.

Pulling myself out of rock-bottom took a year of rehab. I live with the guilt of that every day. As well as the guilt of everything else.

There's too much at stake for me to even consider drowning in my misery like I did before. I've just inherited immeasurable power. It's time to start using it to get the woman I love back.

Then I can begin making up for everything I allowed to happen to her.

So I stand, button up my dark-gray blazer, and face my uncle. "I'm ready."

chapter 2

<u>andrew</u>
present

i was nineteen-years-old when I graduated from alcohol to drugs. On the exact day that marked the one year anniversary of Lexi's disappearance from my life. My binge only lasted six months; enough time to leave a lasting mark.

It took one car crash and the subsequent realizations that hit me to get my stupid ass to wake up.

I was causing my mother pain. Her teary eyes were the first thing I saw upon awakening in the hospital.

The all-body cast encasing my body was the second.

That's when my next realization slid into place: I would never find Lexi if I ended up killing myself.

Her and my mother's faces got me through the next year of therapy, when I had to wait for my body to heal, and had to relearn how to use my legs properly.

All while battling to break free from a heroin addiction and being forced to face the demons that caused them in therapy.

That's how much that girl came to mean to my pathetic, egocentric, sixteen, seventeen, eighteen . . . and nineteen-year-old self.

I'm lying. She meant that much to me way before.

Since the beginning.

You're not supposed to know what romantic love feels like as a child.

I'm pretty sure I knew.

And that's how much she still means to the twenty-five-year-old man I've become. The man that's about to use all his resources and break at least five federal laws, if not more, to locate her.

Step one: befriend the new head of the IT department so that she'll make sure the employees overlook what I plan to do with the systems.

Why am I thinking about this, even when I know I shouldn't allow myself to, at least not until I'm closer to actually implementing the first step of my plan?

The elevator doors I'm standing in front of are a gray steel that's messing with my head.

Reminding me of gray eyes staring up at me, hazy with pleasure.

A bolt of heat slashes right through my nervous system, igniting my heart.

Ah, fuck. My dick is hard and I'm in an elevator, next to my uncle.

"The new head of our IT department is one of the best, Drew."

Beautiful. My uncle decides to start speaking to me while I struggle to get my body back under control.

Trust me, the last thing you want to hear when your cock is pounding is a relative's voice. Much less your *uncle's* voice.

"Mmhm," I mumble, staring down at the marble floor. I can't keep staring at the steel in front of me.

Not if I want to meet this new super-nerd my uncle hired without my dick standing straight and tall before her face.

Mother of Shit. Even thinking the word "nerd" is too much for me to handle right now.

"We managed to steal her from Menahan Industries," my uncle continues, voice brimming with pride.

Deservedly so. Menahan—that little bastard—is our direct competition. Luring one of his employees away had to have been expensive as hell, not to mention legally complicated.

An impressive feat.

I can't formulate any type of response though.

Big gray eyes, framed by those thick black glasses I loved, had locked on mine that night, showing me every emotion I caused in her.

Every emotion I *owned*.

Her brow had scrunched from the pleasure I gave her, her lips parted, begging me to take them.

To take everything.

"Andrew! Oh . . . you're . . . I'm coming . . . uh!"

Fuck, her cries. As long as I live, I'll never forget them. Those sweet little moans still have the power to make me come harder than any woman ever has, even though they only exist within my memories now.

Lexi came all over my thigh that night.

Then my fingers.

It hadn't been enough. I attacked her again later, eating her out on the hood of my car, under the stars, and the experience fucked with me on a molecular level. Forcing her thighs open, I made her drench my tongue, her walls sucking me in deeper and deeper with each orgasm I gave her.

I still remember every freaking facet of her taste. What it felt like to have her swollen little clit in my mouth.

But she hadn't come all over my dick. There hadn't been a chance.

I lost her the very next morning.

"Andrew? Are you listening to me? Are you alright?"

No, I'm not. Haven't been for so long now that I'm starting to wonder if I ever really was.

Do I even have a clue what "normal" feels like?

"I'm fine. Just a lot on my mind."

My uncle nods as we exit the elevator on the lowest floor of the building, where the IT department is located. "It's a lot to take in at once. I know. These introductions are necessary though."

I don't dispute that, because he's right. At this point we've visited every department, made sure everyone has seen the face of their new boss. My uncle has been around much longer than I, so he's well known.

Feared in his own right.

Respected.

Oddly enough, also well-liked despite all that.

His introducing me to everyone is a strategic business move. I'm the son of a man that wasn't known for being the best type of person. If I'm going to keep the board under control, I have to make myself invaluable to the company.

I have to become everything my uncle is, and more. Employee fealty goes a long way to helping a CEO retain their position of power.

But as I follow my uncle down the marble and steel hallway, I'm having a moment of utter weakness. One of many throughout my adult life.

The latch in my mind is busted wide open, the door barely hanging on by its hinges. There is no barrier between myself and the memories.

One in particular comes on strong. It's the one that kills me the most. The full, amazing, *bitter* recollection of what happened the first night I tasted her.

The night that would lead to my losing her.

The night she'd been mine in every sense but the one that mattered most.

chapter 3

andrew

7 years ago

i think Stephen is starting to suspect what I'm really coming to his step-dad's gym for.

Sure, it seems like he's bought into my lie of wanting to practice on my own. It's not like I haven't done it before. For years, I've found random places—anywhere I can hang my punching bag from—and spent hours going at it by myself.

Practicing my uppercuts, jabs, haymakers, roundhouse kicks. Tearing my body down physically so I won't have to deal with any of the mental shit I've got going on.

Everyone at school sees me as some type of warrior. A prized fighter even though I don't fight professionally.

I never will. My father would kill me if I even mentioned stepping into the ring.

At school, the "official" sport I play is football. After school,

Stephen, Barnard, and I practice mixed martial arts. It's our thing. Stephen's uncle owns an MMA studio, and that's where we hang a lot of the time.

If I'm not practicing on my own, as I said.

My friends know I've got some kind of issues. They don't have the details, but obviously something has to be wrong with me if I insist on spending large periods of time by myself.

Yeah, I'm aware. The irony isn't lost on me. I hear the whispers. One of the most popular guys in school is actually a closet loner.

Bite me.

Father pisses me the fuck off on a daily basis. Sometimes two or three times a day.

I rather be by myself when I work through the anger. Pushing my body to the max, exhausting myself, is the only true outlet I have.

Breaking Father's face would be lovely, but mother has already instilled in me how wrong that would look to everyone we know.

Always keep up appearances and all that.

So when I told Stephen I wanted late night access—as in: "Get me the fucking keys"—to his step-dad's gym, he seemed to have no problem saying yes.

That was three weeks ago and everything seemed cool.

Until today. Earlier, when Stephen asked me if I was going to use the gym tonight, I could've sworn I saw an odd glint in his eyes.

Maybe it's just my guilt superimposing shit, though. Because I *am* lying to him about why I come to the gym.

I'm sure you've guessed by now that it has nothing to do with working out.

Every night, after ten, I sneak out of my house, drive two miles to the gym, and meet up with a girl.

Not just any girl either.

A girl that used to be my best friend, back when we were kids.

A girl who lost her father and family stability because my father is sometimes the legend of Mephistopheles made manifest.

A girl that lights me up so hard, like nothing else in the world can.

A girl that *isn't* my girlfriend.

This is all so fucked up.

Don't get me wrong. I'm not cheating on my girlfriend with Lexi.

Do I want to?

Hell no. What I really want to do is dump Kaylee so I can be with Lexi. That's what I fucking want.

Can it happen?

Do humans have the ability to magically sprout wings and *fly*?

Apparently, I wasn't born to have anything I want. Fuck my free will, or any possible desires born from it. It's all about what my father wants for me.

He has my entire destiny mapped out.

I approached him last week, letting him know I planned to leave Kaylee.

And why.

I know. Stupid me, right?

His words . . . Man, they made me want to break shit.

"Kaylee is a Whittacker, boy. Clearly, you're as stupid as I always figured you were. You want to leave a Whittacker for a Berkman? Did you forget what I did to her father when he thought he could get in my way? Do I have to get rid of her too? Or are you just doing this to prove to me what a disappointment you truly are?"

Ah. My father. King of the Assholes.

Here's the thing: I'd leave Kaylee any way if Lexi showed me even a hint of interest. Like *that*.

I've seen small glimpses, little things here and there that make me believe . . . If I'm going to go up against my father, make Lexi his target, I need to know for sure.

There can be no doubt.

All I think about is her wanting me back. Being with her. It keeps me up at night, messes with my concentration at school.

A never-ending secret fantasy since the girl started developing into a woman.

I slide the key into the lock, opening the back door of the gym, all the while shaking my head at myself.

chapter 4

andrew

7 years ago

It's normal that I want Lexi as much as I do, you know? She's always been one of the nerds; no living, breathing guy with a functioning dick gives a fuck.

Lexi chose early on in the sixth grade to alienate herself from the popular kids in school. Back then, we'd called them every infantile name in the book. Nerds. Losers.

I say "we", because thanks to my father's social circle, I was drafted into the popular crew the moment I stepped foot in middle school.

Even back then, Lexi was adorable. Round, gray eyes. Full pink lips. Those big, blonde curls falling over her shoulders.

No wonder she grew up into what most guys at school have dubbed "the Destroyer." Adorable isn't the only adjective she can proudly claim. Her style isn't particularly In-Your-Face sexy—something

Kaylee and her clique love to tease Lexi about relentlessly—but nothing in the world can hide that type of attractiveness.

It's blatant. Wild. Leaks into every part of her personality, so that just the sound of her breathing leaves you panting in response.

Watching her walk leaves you a throbbing, pre-coming mess.

Hearing her voice keeps you up all night, jacking off back to back, because you can't stop imagining what it'd be like to hear her moan your name.

I'm sure you can guess the real reason Kaylee and all her friends despise Lexi. They know damn well that all the guys at school walk around in a haze of sexual fantasies, all thinking about the one girl that doesn't even try to get their attention.

Nerds, emo-fucks, and jocks alike are ready to prostrate themselves at Lexi's feet, *sans* clothing, if she would so much as smile in their direction.

Anger sparks at the thought. As always. I can't deal with that reality. Hate ruminating on how the other guys want her as much as I do. That shit drives me crazy in ways even my father can't.

Pushing it all aside, I glance at the purple gift bag I'm holding as I walk into the gym.

It's Lexi's eighteenth birthday today.

I never forgot the day her birthday falls on. Not even after we were separated at ten.

I'm early, so I get busy turning on the lights in the back office. I place my book bag on the side table. Last second, I decide to hide the giftbag on the floor, behind the couch.

I want to surprise her.

Unzipping my bag, I pull out my advanced computer science textbook. Lexi thinks I'm failing that class.

I'm not.

Yes, I lied to her about that. Don't think I'm not aware that I have more of my father in me than is healthy. Unlike my father, however,

I am capable of feeling guilt.

And I do. Every day that she sneaks out of her house to come meet me, because she thinks I'm failing a subject that I'm actually passing.

With honors.

Why did I lie to her?

Why does anyone ever lie? Either because they're trying desperately to get out of a situation, or because they want something so bad they're willing to risk that age-old threat of eternal hell to get it.

The opportunity presented itself, longing choked the ever-living fuck out of me, and I couldn't fight the impulse to take it.

For years, I watched my old friend from afar, missing her. Knowing what my father had done to her family. I just wanted to have the right to talk to her again.

When that aforementioned opportunity popped up, no preternatural, Zeus-gifted willpower could have stopped me from taking it.

The door creaks open out in the hall. "Andrew?"

God—Nature—whatever the fuck is out there—what the hell did you do when you allowed that girl to come into existence?

Ungh, that voice. I freeze on the spot, eyes closing. Hating and savoring the heat that drums through my veins, pounding its way straight to my cock.

Her voice is how I imagine an ancient sex goddess' voice would've been. If this is how the ancient Sumerians imagined that Inanna's voice sounded, no wonder man eventually rose up and obliterated her legend.

No female, even a mythical one, should be allowed to have so much control over man.

It's not an exaggeration, either. Every fucker at school goes glossy-eyed whenever Lexi so much as hums near them.

The perfect soft rasp; the epitome of the term "sex voice". Every time she says my name, I die a little more inside.

"Andrew?"

Shit. I need to hear her moan for me—don't care if it ends up being the death of me—and I can't fucking have it.

One day I'm going to snap and take it anyway.

"Andrew, are you here?"

I clear my throat, sitting down on the sofa as fast as I can. My text book gets positioned just right, so that it covers my aching hard-on. "Yeah. I'm in here."

Jesus, talk about rasps. My voice is straight up laden with sex.

I clear my throat again.

Three deep breaths, and I convince myself that I'm ready to face her. That, although my dick still throbs to the beat of her name, I'm well on my way to getting my reaction under control.

She stops in front of the door.

My entire world grinds to a halt.

Jesus.

Air . . . Can't breathe . . . Motherfuck, this hurts.

My.

Fucking.

God.

Son of a bitch.

Shit, I think I'm wheezing.

Legs.

Those breasts.

That hair.

The eyes.

Red lips.

Lexi all dolled-up—no, fuck that, *sexed*-up.

Like I've never seen her before.

It's the hardest blow of my life.

And, it's the exact moment in time I realize that girl *has* to be mine.

Whatever it takes.

Whatever it ends up costing me.

Mine.

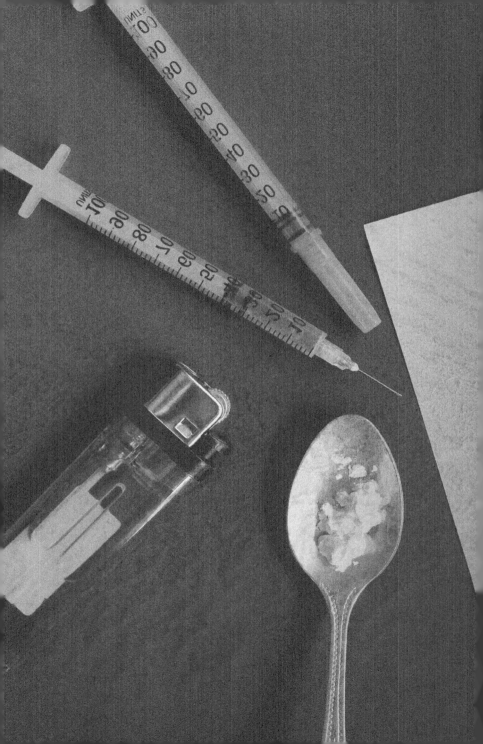

chapter 5

andrew

7 years ago

"h-hey," Lexi murmurs softly, shifting from foot to foot. Probably nervous because I'm staring at her like a brain-dead idiot.

My mind is the complete opposite of dead right now. Thoughts race, flying. Cataloging. Processing every delicious inch of what stands before me.

Lexi usually wears jeans. Button downs. Sensible cardigans. Converses, or boots in the winter.

None of that is in sight right now.

No, she isn't naked. Lord in Heaven, I don't think I'd survive seeing her without clothes.

I'm barely surviving what I'm seeing now.

That bright blue dress hugs everything. Tiny straps wrap around her shoulders, and the low cut, square neckline has a two-inch slit in the middle that clearly shows off her cleavage.

No way she's wearing a bra under there.

Her cute little feet are encased in black flats.

I knew she has a hot body, but fuck. Me.

That *body*.

I can't fucking deal right now, and her face just makes it all so much worse. My heart pumps like crazy and I tell myself to look away.

I fail.

It's bad.

I eat her up with my eyes. Those big blonde curls I'm so fixated with frame her face, her shoulders, falling all the way down her back.

My heart punches hard against my ribcage again, angry at me for denying it what's before me—for subjecting it to the sight of so much beauty.

Her eyes are highlighted by black eyeliner, framed by even darker, thick eyelashes. The look in them tells me that I'm doing it, I'm giving it all away, she can see how much I want her, clear as fucking day.

I can't stop.

The same lips I dream of sucking on, stained by dark red lipstick, become so much more to me.

Those are the lips I breathe for.

The lips I'd kill for.

In the future, I will do wrong, dark, evil things for this girl. To myself and to others.

And those lips will be a big part of the reason why.

A wild, primitive hunger roars inside my gut, demanding its due. "Jesus, you look fucking beautiful," I growl out, too lost in the affect she has on me to even try and hide how I feel right now.

Beastly.

Deranged.

Like I'm two seconds from picking her up and flinging her onto this couch, so I can pin her to it and rub my dick over every inch of her.

"Thank you," she tells me, breathless.

That voice hits me like a lick across my cock. I force my body not to move a single fucking muscle, because if it does, it's going to do what it wants to do and head straight to her.

Lexi steps into the office, hands fidgeting.

I'm making her nervous.

Shit, I'm making myself nervous. I have no clue what I'm going to do next, if I'll be able to rein in my impulses. "Why are you dressed like that?"

Not that it's any of my business, but the thought occurs to me that she might be dressed up like that because she's planning on going out.

She looks like a girl would look when heading out on a date.

Fuck that. That shit *is* my business. "Why?" I demand again, ready to jump off the couch and block her way back out.

"I . . . some of my new friends convinced me to celebrate."

I can tell by her expression that she thinks I don't know why she should be celebrating. My mind gets stuck on her mention of "new" friends and I rake my memory for any clue as to who they might be.

Last week, I remember her hanging out with some of the chess crew. She was talking in the hallway with two girls . . . and two guys.

Two dorks that looked like they were seconds away from busting a load, just because she stood near them and spoke to them.

Is that who she's going out with?

An eerie stillness falls over me. I have no right to feel jealous over a girl that isn't mine.

Which tells me everything I need to know. This one *is* mine. Or, to be more exact, I'm hers.

Shit, I've known that for months now. It's why I went to my

father and let him know I'm leaving Kaylee.

For her.

For Lexi.

Fuck my father's consent. I'm doing it. I'm claiming this girl. Because thinking of her going out there, looking that beautiful, being herself, and some other asshole picking her up, making her feel special, *dating* her, makes me violent.

I'm going to have her.

But first, I gotta make sure she's going to be okay about it.

Holding her stare, I let the textbook fall onto the couch next to me and I get to my feet. Slow. My movements echo the stillness that still surrounds me. That unerring, calm certainty that I know heralds something more.

chapter 6

andrew
7 years ago

If she reacts to me that way I hope she does, I have no idea exactly how I'm going to respond. All I know for sure is that there won't be anything slow, still, or calm about it.

Lexi blinks behind her glasses, her hands falling to her sides. Her eyes are locked on mine.

Her chest trembles with a shuddering breath.

The muscles of my back ripple with that breath. I clench my fists. My chest tenses.

She does it again, as if somehow feeding off what I feel.

Suddenly, it's too damn hot in here. I rip off my windbreaker, leaving me in only my gray t-shirt.

Lexi's eyes widen, then drop down the length of my body.

Fuck. I'm so ready for her.

Please tell me this means she's ready for me.

I cross the distance between us in four strides, taking my time, each step methodical.

I'm giving her a chance. Letting her see me stalk toward her. What I plan to do when I get there.

That I'm waiting for her to open her mouth and protest.

She doesn't.

And I'm in front of her now, head angled down to stare at her because she's so short compared to me.

She tilts her head back to stare at me.

Her chest trembles again.

My fingers twitch with the need to grab her, haul her against me. By sheer force of will, I reach up slowly, giving her even more time to pull away.

She'll never know how much it costs me. How hard it is for me to not just grab her like I want.

Like not breathing even though you're suffocating. Like refusing a piece of steak after starving for over a week.

Her throat moves with a swallow, but she doesn't move away. She remains there, still, waiting for me.

Fuck.

I cup her face in my hands.

Her lids flutter but she doesn't let them close, those eyes going cloudy on me in a way I've only dreamed of before now.

"Lexi . . ." I let my thumbs move across her soft cheeks.

Her lashes flutter again.

Lightning courses through my veins because this is it. This is the reaction I'd hoped for, *prayed* for, the one I knew deep down I was going to fucking get.

All I want to do is eat that juicy mouth of hers; somehow I keep myself under a tight leash.

One that is quickly loosening, seconds away from breaking.

"Happy birthday," I breath, my vision hazy from the force of my hunger for her.

Her eyes widen.

She thought I forgot. That I didn't know.

I caress her cheeks with my thumbs one more time. "I never forgot," I tell her softly, teeth grinding against each other.

Those pretty cheeks go pink, and her eyes shine with a mixture of confusion, shock, and delight.

That's when I get worried. That glow in her eyes tears through the last of my self control. I waited years for her to talk to me again. To let me back into her life.

It seems like I waited my whole fucking life for her to stare up at me like that, with that little pleased look in her eyes.

Now that I have it, a force rips through me, one more powerful than I anticipated.

I'm meant to put that glow in her eyes.

Me.

I'm meant to be that for her. I know this more than I know my own name right now.

I'm meant to own this woman, every emotion in her, every ounce of her happiness.

Her body.

Holy fuck, *yes*. I'm going to have that body. I'm going crazy just thinking about it, but somehow I keep myself there.

I got my reaction. I can start exploring this attraction between us.

But I can't do what my body wants. I want to fuck her right on the couch behind me. Then I want to fuck her on the side table that's up against the wall.

Lexi isn't that type of girl. Not to me. She deserves for me to date her, make her my girl before I fuck her.

"Thank you." Lexi nuzzles the palm of my hand.

I force myself to let go because I want to fucking eat her and I can't. "I . . . got you something." Turning, I head over to grab the gift bag off the floor.

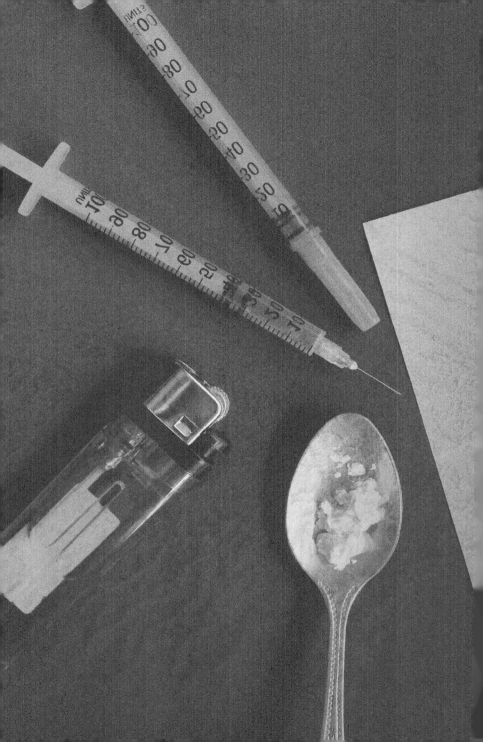

chapter 7

<u>andrew</u>
7 years ago

"**Y**ou did?"

The surprise in her tone rubs me the wrong way. I resolve to give her things as often as possible from now on. She'll never be surprised again that I got her something.

When I straighten, Lexi is there, standing in front of the couch. She looks all excited, nervous—delicious in every way that counts.

I sit on the couch, holding the purple bag.

It's her favorite color. Always has been.

Wonder if she picks up on the fact that I still remember that, too.

"Come here." I watch hungrily as she slowly eases down onto the couch next to me. "It isn't anything huge, or crazy. It's something small, actually. I wanted to get you something I knew you would like—"

She cuts off my rambling. "Andrew. Give it to me." Lexi smirks at me and holds out her hand.

It's a sad, sad fact that while I stare at her outstretched hand, the gift bag is the very last thing I want to give her. Well, I do want to give it to her, but first, I want her to hold something else. A part of my body.

And not just the obvious part, either. I'd be happy just having her small hand wrapped around my own.

Ah, shit. That's more than sad. It borders on pathetic. What the hell is this girl turning me into?

Oh, but I know. Don't fucking like it; can't fucking fight it.

"Drew?"

She hasn't called me by that nickname since we were kids.

I go hot at the sound of it. So freaking hot. *Blazing.* The urge to rip off my clothes is ridiculous.

"Here." I hand her the bag and brace my elbows on my knees, my clenched fists hanging in between. *Don't reach for her. Don't touch her.*

For the first time, I honestly hope Lexi isn't a virgin. I'm not going to be able to be gentle with her once I'm in her.

She reaches into the bag. Her brow scrunches when she pulls out the wooden box in it. She turns it around and her eyes widen when she spots the necklace hanging inside, right in front of the Harry Potter logo etched into the small mirror.

Her shocked eyes lock on mine. "Drew," she gasps.

Don't fucking touch her.

I clench my fists harder.

"You got me a time turner?" Her low, tender tone makes her voice sound even sexier.

And makes me feel like I'm the most accomplished motherfucker walking the Earth.

See? Told you. It's my job to put that happy little look on her face and her reaction right now just proved it.

I barely stop myself from puffing out my chest like some cocky loser. "Well, it was either that, or Hermoine's wand," I tell her. "And I saw it hanging out of your bag the other day. So . . . knew you had it."

Lexi opens the box with shaking hands and brings the necklace out. The chain glints in the light. I made sure to get her a custom-made, gold version of the necklace. No way I was getting her the fake shit.

"How did you know I love Harry Potter? Just because you saw the wand?" She doesn't look up at me, eyes still glued on the necklace in her hand.

Which is fine by me, like that she can't see the look on my face when I answer, "No. It's because I pay attention to you. A lot of it."

Our eyes lock again.

"Drew . . . " She stops and swallows heavily.

What does that look in her eyes mean? Damn it, *what*?

"Thank you so much."

I open my mouth to respond—

Lexi leans forward and presses a kiss right against the corner of my lips.

chapter 8

andrew
present

my uncle clearing his throat rips me from the memory. I feel the loss of it so acutely that I want to push him into the wall for taking it from me.

He didn't, actually. It's still there, etched into every piece of my mind, lurking. As always. All I need to do is turn my attention to it, just a little, and I'll be overcome again. Transported right back to that night.

I can't. My uncle is standing in front of a set of large doors that lead into the main lab of the applied sciences division; a branch of our IT department.

However, we strictly develop hardware in this part of the department, something only a select few people know right now. We're planning on taking the market by storm.

That explains the need for the handprint and retinal scanner next to the doors.

"Drew?" My uncle waves at the scanner. He doesn't bother to ask the question that I once again see in his eyes: *Are you alright?*

I step up to the scanner and place my hand on it, then bend slightly to let it scan my eye next. My uncle has the same level of clearance I have—absolute—but he wants me to get used to doing all this by myself.

Not that small shit like this is difficult, but it was never my intention to take over this company—that is, until the day I realized it'd be the perfect revenge against my father—and I made that very clear to everybody after I lost Lexi.

My uncle prides himself on being a better father figure to me than his brother was.

He is. Always has been. That's why I let him have his fatherly moments where he gets to show me around and "teach" me everything I need to know.

The doors unlock and we walk inside. I haven't been here in a while and I'm impressed with the set-up now that it's all done. This entire part of the division was completed in less than eight months. Considering the scope and size of it all, and the sheer amount of equipment in here, it's a huge feat.

My uncle nods toward a group of men standing in front of a large LCD.

I follow him over to them, taking in the image on the screen. Python coding stares back at me—one of the main languages in software development.

I don't have enough time to read through all of it but I'm pretty sure the group of men we're approaching are the ones heading the Providence project.

Sure enough. We stop in front of the work station facing the LCD and I spot the large black goggles on top of it.

Rumors leaked late last year that Menahan had begun making their own version of the Oculus Rift, the video gaming goggles currently being developed. The goggles will allow gamers to virtually step into the worlds of the games they play and visually experience them as if they're inside it.

Menahan, that asshole, has no interest in the gaming world. He's into informational theft. He disguises it by presenting his "innovations" to the public as regular security advancements.

But we all know what his clients truly hire him for.

My uncle and I are also very aware who one of Menahan's main targets is going to be.

Us.

That scumbag has a personal vendetta against us.

Against *me*.

That's okay, though. I have an even bigger one against him. He's one of the people that hurt Lexi.

Menahan has no fucking idea what's coming to him.

My uncle makes quick work of introducing me to the group of men surrounding the Providence goggles; mainly, Paul Rundlett, the man leading the entire project. "Paul here is working directly with the head of our IT department. He left Menahan when she left and came to us alongside her."

Paul smiles at me, his blue eyes lighting up at the mention of the new head of IT. "I'd follow that girl anywhere and she knows it. Berkman is a bloody genius and working alongside her is a pleasure."

It's just a name. One that isn't even that unique. He could've been talking about anyone.

Don't ask me how I know it's her. I just do.

My veins go ice cold.

My focus becomes engaged on him and only him.

I'm probably staring at him like a goddamned lunatic but I don't care. "What was that name again?"

Paul blinks. "Uh . . . Berkman? She's the main developer on the Providence software now. Did you get a chance to meet Lexi yet?"

The world spins dangerously. I stagger back, feeling like I've just been hit.

And that's when I catch sight of my uncle's wide eyes and the expression on his face.

chapter 9

<u>andrew</u>
7 years ago

I've been hit many times in my life. Mentally. Emotionally. I'm no stranger to pain in all its myriad forms, have experienced every level of it from a measly one to a devastating ten.

Lexi's lips linger on my skin for a second longer than they should, the corner of her mouth pressed intimately to the corner of mine.

I hear her surprised inhale when she realizes what she's done. She moves to pull away and it hits me: I've never felt this kind of agony before. Nothing's ever come close.

She can't take this away from me.

I won't let her.

My hand snaps around the back of her neck, stopping her. Her face is mere inches from my own. So beautiful that I just want to nuzzle it.

Later. First, I need those lips back on my skin.

"Andrew?" She stares into my eyes, curious.

I see the hunger in her eyes, the one that almost matches my own.

It's enough. A start. I'll make her burn as much as I do by the time I'm through with her.

I lean in and brush the tip of my nose across hers. "I need your lips, Lexi." She will never know how much.

"A-Andrew . . . we shouldn't."

She's so fucking right.

I pluck the necklace out of her hand and blindly dump it back into the gift bag. "Tell me you don't want me to kiss you," I say, staring right into her eyes.

Those glasses she's wearing look so sexy on her.

Somehow, she's keeping them on while I do her. No matter how rough it gets.

Her hands wrap around my shoulders. "I . . . can't say that."

Exactly the answer I expected.

The one I wanted.

God help us both.

"Baby, I'm going to kiss you," I breathe against her lips.

Her last warning. This is her last chance to say no.

Her eyes slide closed.

Groaning, I fit my lips to hers. My entire body jerks at the first, silky contact.

It's like I waited my entire fucking life to feel those lips. Fuck. How did I ever live without this girl's mouth?

I don't press for more, leaving our lips meshed together, taking every breath that leaves her into myself. My blood has never pounded so brutally through my veins; my dick has never been this hard.

I want her tongue more than I want my next breath, but I won't be able to handle feeling it. Not without pinning her beneath me and

TWISTED HEARTBREAK

taking everything she has to give.

Lexi shudders and my body responds with a shudder of its own.

I give her bottom lip one more peck and move back, ending our kiss. I can't go further. Too many things are roaring in my head. Things I need from her that can't happen right now.

She grabs onto my neck, my jaw, bringing me back to her mouth.

Holy shit. I can't resist this.

Her tongue slips inside.

A moan is torn from me, my self-control along with it. I cup her face, my tongue playing wetly with hers.

Lexi. This is fucking Lexi kissing me, and when a small moan leaves her, my entire body reaches a breaking point.

I have to stop kissing her. If I don't, I'm going to fuck her. Right here. I don't even know how far she's gone.

I haven't taken her on a date yet.

She deserves so much better than to be fucked on a couch in the office of a gym.

Lexi latches onto my bottom lip, sucking on it repeatedly. Soothing it with her tongue. Like it's her little play thing.

My pulse explodes everywhere inside me.

"Lexi . . . fuck. Wait," I whisper, too out of breath to speak any louder.

She lets me end our kiss and sits there, panting—eyes heavy-lidded, cheeks pinks, lips swollen from my kisses.

Oh God. My fucking cock hurts so bad. I want her hands on it. *Now.*

Suddenly, she gasps, a horrified expression taking over her face. Her hand flies up, fingertips pressing to the lips I just kissed. "Shit. What did I just do? God. I'm sorry. Why'd I do that? You have a girlfriend!" She shoots off the couch.

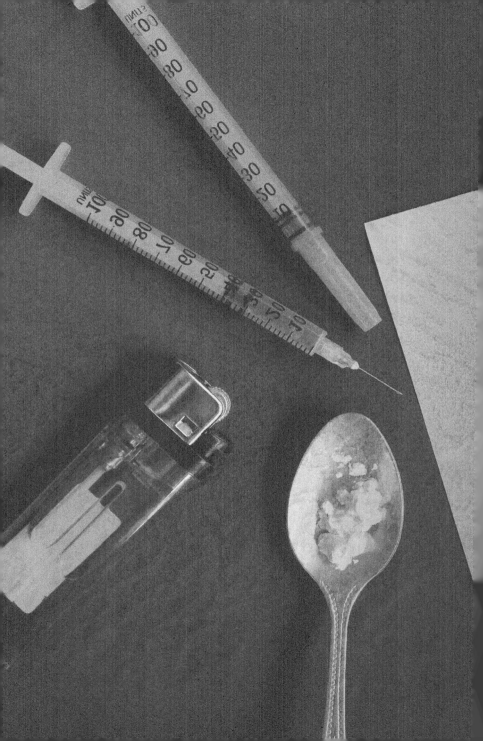

chapter 10

<u>andrew</u>
7 years ago

i jump up after her.

Lexi paces across the small office space. "Stupid. I'm so stupid. Why would I do something like that?"

I grab her shoulders. "Listen to me. Stop blaming yourself. *I* kissed you."

"Why did you?"

That's a question I definitely shouldn't answer. Not here. Not under these circumstances.

I have no choice. Her big eyes remain on mine, waiting for an answer, and they're both curious and vulnerable.

Us guys? We play with girls. That's what we do. Girls hate us for it, but most are so desperate to have us in their lives that they let us get away with anything. With women being so willing to forgive us, why should we change?

This isn't the first time I've cheated on Kaylee. Hell, no. She knows I have, too. Oh, she was furious when she found out, but she came chasing after *me* when I tried to end it.

But Lexi . . . if she were my girl, I wouldn't play with her, cheat on her.

Shit. I really wouldn't. The thought of hurting her in any way makes me sick.

God help me. I think I love this girl.

Shaken by that revelation—and feeling absolutely fucking stupid because I'm just admitting this now—I cup her face.

Fuck. I hope she can't tell that my hands are trembling.

"I . . . " Have no idea what to tell her without divulging what it is that I really feel for her. Too soon for that. At the very least though, I can go with some honesty. I don't like the idea of her thinking I'm just playing with her. "I like you, Lexi. Have for a while. When I felt your lips . . . I just couldn't stop myself."

Her eyes soften momentarily.

My thumbs twitch on her cheeks, aching to smooth over her skin.

But I won't take more. I refuse. There's things that have to be straightened out first before I can have her mouth again.

A fact that's driven home with her next statement.

"You have a girlfriend." She moves to step back.

Away from me.

I drop my hands to her shoulders, shaking my head. "I'm only with her because my father wanted it."

Her expression darkens at the mention of my father.

I don't blame her. "I'm leaving her. I even told my father. He knows it's you I want."

At that, her face goes pale. "Andrew, your father hates my family."

My father has no real reason to hate her family—but he's always

TWISTED HEARTBREAK

been good at deluding himself like that. He's fucked you over? Easy fix. All he has to do is convince himself that you somehow deserved what you got. It's all your fault. He's just the victim lashing out in the name of retaliation.

He'll go after Lexi and her mother if *I* get in the way of his plans to unite our family with Kaylee's. That's what Lexi's afraid of. She doesn't have to say it out loud; I thought it, too.

I drop my hands to grab hers. "I know, and I'm sorry. I shouldn't have told him why I'm leaving Kaylee. I just—forget it." Pressing my lips together, I stop myself before I can go further, realizing how pointless this is right now.

Until I'm officially single, I can't be completely honest with Lexi. It wouldn't be fair to her.

But she doesn't let it go.

I kind of expected she wouldn't.

"You just what, Andrew?"

She hasn't pulled her hands out of mine, letting me rub my thumbs into her skin, and I take comfort in that.

"Andrew?"

I sigh, giving in. There's no way I can resist telling her the truth. At least part of it. "All I could think about was being single so I could ask you on a date."

She arches her eyebrow, making me smile. "Just to ask me on a date?"

My smile widens. "To start."

Her eyes flicker over my face, pausing at my mouth.

"And when I start dating you, Lexi, I'm not fucking hiding you from anybody."

Her juicy lips part and my cock throbs painfully for them.

Soon, I'll have those lips all over my naked body. Wrapped around the swollen tip of my dick.

I throb in my shorts again at the thought, my tip slick against my briefs. Tightening my hands around hers, I breathe through the rush of desire, reminding myself that I'm doing the right thing by waiting. I've never waited for a girl. Never had to. This shit is already proving to be harder than I thought it was going to be. I've never done "right" by a girl. I want to with her. The reminder is the only thing that keeps me steady.

She wiggles her fingers, signaling that she wants me to let her hands go. I do, but it takes a shitload more effort than is normal. Smoothing her hands across my shoulders, Lexi steps closer, looking up at me with those sexy, open, vulnerable eyes that somehow scream at me to *do her.*

My body shoots tight with tension.

"Are you serious right now? Or are you just playing with me?" she asks softly.

I growl under my breath, angry that she would even think I'd do her like that. "Lexi, I want you to listen to me and listen well." Pinching her chin, I make her stare into my eyes. "I've never wanted anything as much as I want you. And I'm damn well prepared to do anything I have to do to have you."

chapter 11

<u>andrew</u>
7 years ago

i expected her to react to that comment a million different ways. With disbelief. Anger. Maybe even fear.

Imagine my shock when she steps even closer, pressing every inch of her body against mine.

Heat flares everywhere. Inside my body. Outside it. In the air that crackles with pure electricity around us.

Her thin arms come around my neck and she lays her head on my chest, right above my raging heartbeat. Snuggling into me, she gives me the sweetest hug I've ever been given.

There's nothing sexual about this hug—well, unless you count the fact that I'm hard as freaking steel, and her abs are pressed right against my cock.

I hear what might be her surprised gasp, but she doesn't pull away. No. She snuggles into me again, her head tucked under my chin in the most adorable way. I wrap my arms around her, returning her hug.

She gives me a happy little sigh.

God, she makes my fucking chest ache.

I duck my head and press my nose to her hair, inhaling her scent.

Her arms tighten around me. "Thank you for the gift, Drew. I love it."

There are no words. A simple "you're welcome" won't suffice. The necklace is such a small thing, incomparable to all the things I want to give her, but I'm glad it's made her happy.

I've spent years of my life watching those big eyes sadden from afar. Knowing my asshole of a father was largely responsible.

Lexi tilts her head back, letting me see her eyes, shining exactly like I need them to—*happily*. Her hands slide down, smoothing over the gray t-shirt I'm wearing. An innocent move on her part, I know this.

My skin flares, every cell responding to that touch.

I want to fuck. I want to come.

With her.

Thrusting into her savagely, her wet tight pussy squeezing the come right out of me, the scent of all that wetness so deep in me that it'll become all I can smell and taste.

Jesus.

I don't even want to try with any other girl. My mind is fixated on how fucking amazing it'd be to have her.

Knowing that I can't aggravates the hell out of me. I will, someday, but until that day comes, I need to keep my distance. Being this close to her is too much of a tease.

I start to move back.

Her hands fist around my shirt.

Lexi's refusal to let me go scatters every single thought in my head, leaving only the haze.

I swear to God my vision's tunneling. That's how hot she makes me.

My shaking hands wrap tightly around her fists.

She tightens her hold before I can remove them. "Andrew . . . I shouldn't."

"What?" The heat in her eyes confuses me—turns me on more. I want her legs shaking on either side of my head. Her body wrapped around every inch of mine. It's all I can think about.

Her little hands are wrapped so tightly around my shirt that I'll have to use force to remove them.

And I fucking love it.

Subconsciously, I know what she's about to do, seconds before she does it.

Logic tells me to move back. Break her hold and put some distance between us before she comes at me.

I don't want her to be the girl I cheated on Kaylee with—one of many.

I want Lexi to be so much more than that.

My body doesn't care.

In this moment, neither does she.

I have a split second to react. See her standing on her tiptoes. Feel her little hand wrap around the back of my neck to pull my head down.

A split second where I could've stopped her.

Hell, no. I let her.

I'm too fucking starved to deny her, although I know we'll probably end up hating ourselves once it's over.

Her tongue comes out to play with mine. Wet. Delicious. Anxious.

I respond to her desperation like I've been trained to, every nerve igniting with full force.

Letting go of her shoulders, I slide my hands down the sexy

curve of her back, groaning into our kiss. My hands latch onto her ass, squeezing tight.

She moans into my mouth, pressing closer.

God, my dick is so freaking hard. I nibble her lip and open my eyes—hers are already open, heavy-lidded, watching me.

Ah, shit. I lock eyes with her and an orgasm trembles through my cock. "Lexi," I pant her name, my chest heaving. "You gotta stop now, baby, or—"

She presses her hands to my shoulders and begins leading me backwards. "I want it, Drew."

chapter 12

andrew

7 years ago

morality can be one hell of a strong driving force. It can push you out of the driver's seat, take complete control of the steering wheel and hijack the GPS that decides in which direction your life is going to go.

But it's nothing—absolutely *nothing*—when pitted against desire. Especially one that's been fed for years, an ache that's grown stronger every second it was denied what it wants.

Lexi is that for me. The ideal. The unattainable fantasy that's finally being attained.

She leads me straight back to the couch and I let her. There's no choice but to allow her. She's gripping that steering wheel tight in her hands.

I have no clue where she's taking this—me—but I'll let her do whatever she wants with me.

I'm hers.

She might as well have one hand wrapped around my cock as she leads me; that's how absolute her control over me is right now.

I should be worried over how easily she's grabbed control of me. I'm not. As long as her hands are on me, anywhere, that's all that matters to me.

The back of my legs hit the couch. She pushes down on my shoulders. I fall onto it, eyes on her. My hands itch to reach for her, feel that ass again. I fist them, almost shaking with the effort of keeping my self-control engaged.

I've never done drugs, but I'm sure this is what the craving is like. The hunger that carves out little pieces of your soul.

I let her see it, all of it, even as I fight with myself to remain seated and let her do this at her own pace.

When she urges me to sit back on the couch and sits sideways on my lap, a low sound of desperation breaks out of me.

"Is this okay?" she whispers in that sexy voice of hers, her perfect ass perched on my lap, her eyes on mine, wide and questioning behind those glasses.

I snap.

One hand slides around the back of her neck. The other clamps down around her exposed thigh.

I have her in my hands. Right where I fucking want her.

She launches herself at me at the same time I move toward her, and then it's just our lips—touching. Meshing. Sucking. She lets me play slowly with her tongue, even though I sense the impatience mounting within her.

I press harder, rubbing her tongue with mine roughly. Caressing the side of her neck gently, I swallow every whimper she gives me. Every moan. The hand around her thigh twitches, aching to move closer to the one thing I want the most in the world.

I bite down on the mad urge. Control is essential right now.

Beyond necessary. One wrong move, and I'll have her under me, my cock deep inside her.

Lexi rips her lips away from mine, gasping my name in a needy tone that nearly ruins me. Her hips move restlessly on my thigh. I hiss, clenching my teeth.

Then she goes for my neck, latching onto it, all lips, teeth, and tongue, and I forget about self-control.

I've been kissed, sucked, and tongued by so many girls. I could never count them. Almost every inch of my body.

But if you asked me right now what those girls felt like, I wouldn't be able to tell you jack-shit about it. I don't remember.

She bites on my jugular, moaning around my skin, and oh . . . *fuck*. I can't take it. Can't deal.

I palm the back of her head, tilting my own to offer her more of my neck. "Bite. Harder," I growl, the hand on her thigh bringing her closer. Right onto my cock.

My hips churn desperately, rubbing it into her.

Lexi sucks on me. *Hard.* Like she's trying to leave a mark on me.

God. I'm going to cream my basketball shorts. "Baby . . . what are you doing to me?"

"Drew, I want—" Her voice breaks off on another moan.

Me. My girl wants me.

Rising, I deposit Lexi on the couch, her head against the armrest. One knee braced on the couch, I lean over her, breathing hard.

From the moment we first became friends all those years ago, I've been fixated on that hair. Her eyes.

They watch me now, heavy-lidded, desire hot inside those gray depths. Her big curls are all over the place, framing that pretty face of hers, falling down over her shoulders and around her breasts.

The rapid rise and fall of her chest turns me on even more, and I know my cock's clearly visible through the thin material of my basketball shorts. I want her eyes on it. Her hands. Her lips. That perfect, wet tongue.

As if sensing my thoughts, her eyes drop down, widening when they land on my engorged dick.

I thumb her bottom lip, pressing into it. Probably harder than I should, but I'm barely controlling myself. It's like she's in my fucking blood, a scorching, violent hum I can't fight.

I won't be able to be gentle with her.

I shouldn't touch her like that. Shouldn't run the risk of fucking her, until I'm balls deep, like a crazed, violent brute.

There's no stopping myself.

Parting her lips, I slide my thumb into her, skimming across her bottom teeth. "You want me, baby?"

Her enthusiastic nod is so fucking cute.

"You want my cock?"

She arches, moaning.

My jaw pulses. My teeth grind together.

My heart, the stupid bastard, feels like it rotates inside my chest, kicking, kicking, demanding I fall on her and make her mine.

I slide my thumb, moist from her mouth, along her jaw. "You wet for me?"

A blush explodes beneath her cheeks, but she nods at me and bites her lip shyly.

I groan, feeling my balls tighten. How heavy they are. I don't need to look down to know there's a wet spot on my shorts, right where my tip is. "I'm wet for you, too."

Her eyes drop right back down, zeroing in and making my dick pulse toward her.

I almost jump when her hand lands on my thigh, above my knee, right where my basketball shorts end. Slowly, she begins sliding it upwards.

"Lexi," I growl out, my thighs trembling harder the closer she gets to my dick. "If you touch it, there's no stopping this."

Her eyes flash. "You better not stop."

"Are you a virgin?"

Her hand stops midway up my thigh. She doesn't answer.

I fight back the desperate need to thrust my hips at her, get her hand where I need it.

"Lexi," I say slowly, because I'm almost one-hundred percent sure that her answer might just drive me mad. "Are you?"

More silence from her.

Come on Lexi, don't do this to me . . .

"Does it matter?" she asks.

I jerk my head in a pathetic semblance of a nod. It matters. It matters so much that even I realize what a fucking hypocrite that makes me, but I've waited so long to have her—claim her—that just thinking that someone else beat me to it pisses me the hell off.

"I am."

A breath of air whooshes out of me. Relief. So much of it that I'm almost lightheaded. *Mine.* "Good. I can't have sex with you tonight, though."

Her mouth opens and I see the protest forming before she even speaks.

Sliding my thigh between her legs, I lower myself onto her. "Don't worry, baby. I'm still going to take care of you."

chapter 13

andrew

present

islam my hand onto the scanner and rush out of the lab as soon as the doors slide open. The world around me threatens to spin.

I don't stop.

Can't.

My entire life got wrecked by the centrifugal force of losing one girl.

It happened without my knowing it. It happened way before I could comprehend it. After years of analyzing the sick, twisted obsession in my veins, I realized it happened the very first time I laid eyes on her.

First day of kindergarten.

That girl became the entire world to me. Fuck that, the center of my universe. Without her, I was thrown completely out of orbit.

I should've found another reason to go on, another reason to live.

I couldn't.

It's impossible. I lived for her back then; I live for her now.

And she's here, in my building, working for my company, her presence pulling me toward her, right back into my proper orbit.

"Drew!"

My uncle.

As far as I know, he never knew what Lexi came to mean to me. He knows I self-destructed at one point, but not the real reason why.

Anger sparks regardless. For the last two days, he's been raving about the new IT girl, and how he stole her away from Menahan—

I freeze, unseeing. Disbelieving.

Lexi was working for Stephen? *Stephen*? One of the bastards responsible for hurting her.

My uncle catches up to me. "Andrew."

I whirl on him. "Did you know who she is when you hired her?" I sound as obsessed as I am. Probably look it, too.

There's astonishment in my uncle's dark eyes, as well as that analytical gleam I've come to know so well. Like he's putting the pieces together and realizing what my reaction's really about. "I know you know her since you were kids."

Know her? I fucking *breathe* for the girl. Closing my eyes, I fight to resist the pull of her presence. I don't know what I'm going to do the moment I see her. If I'll be able to control myself.

I need some answers first.

"She was working for Stephen?"

My uncle hesitates. Most likely has to do with the fact that I haven't opened my eyes and I've lost control of my inner psycho. "Yes. For years we heard rumors of his 'hidden asset', the person responsible for giving his company such a huge technological edge."

Lexi was always a genius. Beyond brilliant. "Why was she working for Stephen?" I almost can't accept this fact. Don't want to.

All these years of searching for her, *dying* for her, and she'd been with Stephen of all people.

Rage burns through my veins.

"I don't know, Andrew. That's something you'll have to ask her," my uncle says.

Oh, I plan to. "How long was she working for him?"

"Andrew—"

"Answer. Me."

"The contract between them went into effect five years ago. It was almost ironclad. It took our legal team months to break through it, as well as some help from Ms. Berkman herself after she managed to hack one of his servers."

Like the pathetic, starving man I am, I latch onto that with every bit of strength inside me. "So she wanted to stop working for him?"

"Yes. Was desperate to get out. She has some sort of vendetta against him. She's going to make a great ally."

I've heard enough.

I have a pretty good idea where the software department is, and I'm almost sure that's where she'll be. This connection with her is like a radar, calling me to her.

My uncle grabs my shoulder, halting me. "Drew, what's going on?"

My entire being shakes with suppressed energy, all of it waiting to be unleashed on one woman. "Remember a few years ago, when I almost died because I was out driving high on heroine?"

"Yes . . ."

"She's the one. The reason I broke down, got into drugs. The reason I almost killed myself." *She's the reason I'm an unhinged asshole.*

"Dear God, Drew. I know what your father did to her father, but I didn't—"

"Where is her office?"

He points at a set of large doors with another retinal and handprint scanner.

Fifty-feet down the hall, in the same direction I was heading.

Shrugging his hand off me, I take off, running straight for those doors.

Straight to Lexi.

chapter 14

andrew

7 years ago

"take care of me?" Lexi asks, blinking up at me, all innocence. Enough of it that I suddenly feel like a piece of shit for what I'm about to do to her.

For a second, I contemplate slowing down. Not going so far with her tonight.

Her hands caress the back of my head, nails scratching my scalp through my short, close-cropped hair. Legs parting, she makes room for me and brings me down to her.

My body covers hers, thigh pressed against the heat of her pussy.

A hiss is ripped out of me. So damn wet. Fuck.

She shifts, like she's aching for me to make her come, rubbing that sweet pussy all over my thigh. "What did you mean by 'take care of me'?"

I rock into her, loving her little gasp when I rub against her clit.

My cock throbs with each glide along the top of her thigh, and I swear I can almost feel her pussy pulsating against me.

Groaning, I drop my forehead on hers, careful not to touch her glasses. "It means I can't fuck you. I'm not taking my girl's virginity on a couch, in the back of a gym. But I'm going to make you feel good, baby. Real fucking good."

Jesus, I'm so fucking hard I probably won't last too long before I come in my shorts.

Lexi lifts her hips, sliding along my thigh again, and I moan at the feel of how wet she is. "If—if you're not going to have sex with me, what are you going to do?"

I want my mouth on her, lapping up every wet inch. I've never been big on eating out girls, but tasting her pussy would drive me wild. Undoubtedly.

Which is exactly why I can't do it to her.

"Do you trust me to take care of you, Lexi?"

She tilts her head back, lips brushing sweetly against mine, and whispers, "Yes."

My heart slams into my ribcage. I'm the son of the man responsible for causing her family so much pain. And, yet, she still trusts me.

Fuck. I really do love her.

"You have no idea how I feel about you," I say, looking right into her eyes.

Not giving her time to react, I lean down the rest of the way and cover her lips with mine.

I could come just sucking on her lips. And damn, she's a quick learner too, her tongue moving in just the right away to send more pleasure slicing through me.

I kiss her slowly, because she's wearing her glasses and I love them. So much that I need her to keep them on while I make her come.

She whimpers into my mouth, and I swear I can taste it. The promise of raging sex behind it. Her hips move impatiently. She's fucking my thigh, taking her pleasure from me, and she tries to kiss me harder.

Lungs tight, my cock so heavy, I somehow find a way to refuse her, keeping that kiss just as slow as before.

Because I've never wanted anything in my God forsaken life as much as I want her, and if I give into the call of her body, I'll end up slamming into her and busting my nut right here.

Lexi's breasts press against my chest. Ripping her mouth away from mine, she throws her head back, arching, groaning. "*Drew.*"

God, who am I kidding? I won't make it inside her. Already too close.

I slide my hand under her, flattening it on her lower back, commanding her rhythm. Making her ride my thigh faster. "You make me so hard it hurts." Rotating my hips, I thrust into her, giving her more of my thigh, letting her feel my swollen dick.

Her throat jumps with her next moan.

Unable to resist it, I latch onto it with my teeth, tugging lightly on the side of her neck.

She cries out, right into my ear, and more precome leaks out of me.

"So good," I groan, licking and sucking on her neck feverishly.

"Drew. Oh God." Arching, she rubs her tits into my chest, her hips moving in circles.

I slip my hands between our bodies, refusing to lift myself away from her. My hands cup her breasts and a hungry, soft mewl leaves her. She moves faster, offering me everything.

The fire in my chest slams into my gut, spreading into every limb.

Infecting my fucking soul.

"Mine," I pant into her ear, tugging the top of her dress down.

The sound of the straps tearing reaches me, but I don't care. Her tits are full, perfect in my hands, her nipples tight. I pinch them and she cries out for me again. "Fucking mine, baby. All of you."

"Yes. Please!"

"Yes, what?" I tongue her earlobe, imagining it's her clit, and play with her nipples at the same time. I lift my head just enough to look down at her, waiting.

Eyes anguished, she shakes her head. Our bodies grind naturally, our rhythm frantic but somehow in sync.

Like we were made to fuck each other.

Her next glide leaves a trail of her juices on my thigh.

Oh, fuck. That's for me. All for me. My shaft kicks, hungry to feel all that wetness. "Come on, Lexi." I lick both my thumbs, eyes on her. She shakes her head again, but fuck it. She doesn't have to admit it aloud. Not right now. Every moan that leaves her proves it.

I use my wet thumbs to play with her nipples, fucking her through our clothes. "I meant what I said. Mine. Whatever it takes Lexi."

"I want you so bad, Drew."

I pinch her nipples, hard, a broken groan rumbling in my chest.

"Andrew! Oh . . . you're . . . I'm coming . . . uh!" Eyes on mine, she locks up, coming like a rocket all over my thigh.

Near blind, desperate, I reach between us, searching . . . searching . . .

My hand slides between her legs, making contact with her over her panties.

Beyond wet.

Soaked.

So damn soaked that barely grazing her leaves my hand drenched.

"Fuck baby," I rasp. "I barely touched you and you squirted all over my thigh. That sweet cunt is trying to mark me, isn't it? Trying to leave your scent on me so that every girl knows I'm yours."

She jerks under me, mewling.

Without thinking, I raise my hand back up to my lips, taking my fingers into my mouth.

Time fucking stops at the first hit of her taste on my tongue.

Luscious.

Sweet.

The most addicting thing that could've ever been created.

Wild, practically snarling around my fingers, I suck them hard, needing more of that taste. Knowing it's never going to be enough.

My cock swells to the breaking point, *pounding.*

"Shit!" At the last second, I manage to pull away from her, landing on the other end of the couch. Hands shaking, I drag my cock out.

One pump of my fist, and my orgasm rides straight up my length, about to explode out the tip.

And I don't stop looking at her. I can't. This orgasm is hers, all hers. I want her to see what she's done to me.

Lexi scrambles to sit up and slaps my hand away, grabbing my cock—

My head falls back, a roar breaking loose.

She pumps my dick, milking me, making me come harder.

"Yours, Lexi," I hear my hoarse voice telling her. "All yours."

Somewhere, I either heard or read that sex is better when you actually have feelings for the person you're doing it with. I can officially say that's true. She just blew my fucking mind.

I came so hard I'm still twitching. Lexi plays with my dick. I'm too sensitive, but I can't bring myself to make her stop. I love that she's touching me. Learning me.

I reach out for her, cupping her neck. It takes a ridiculous amount of effort to lift myself and bring her head toward me, kissing her softly.

She sighs into our kiss.

"You're all mine now, baby. Just like I'm yours," I mumble against her lips. "All mine."

chapter 15

andrew

7 years ago

"I am?"

The sweet way her breath hitches when she asks me that gets to me. I nod at her, because for some reason, my throat's too tight for me to speak, and kiss her pouty lips one more time.

A sound reaches my ears. What sounds like someone moving.

A soft snicker.

I rear back away from Lexi, my head flying around in the direction of the door.

The open door.

No one is there. Not that I can see.

My heart races, senses prickling.

"Andrew?"

I shush her, silently placing my index finger on her lips, and stand. Walking softly, I head toward the door, straining to listen.

And I hear it. Footsteps scurrying away from the door.

I jog to the door, anger rising each millisecond it takes me to get there.

Someone's here.

Someone heard my girl coming.

They probably fucking saw us!

Feeling like a wild animal, ready to tear into anyone and anything, I stop at the door, looking left and right.

No one.

No one on the left, heading toward the back door.

No one on the right, heading toward the main area of the gym.

I heard someone. I know I did.

"Baby, stay here." Jogging, I make my way down the hall and into the main sparring area. It's dark, all the lights out. Seemingly empty.

Yeah right. This place is huge. A person can hide anywhere. It would take me forever to find them.

Still, the thought that someone heard and saw Lexi galvanizes me. I can't rest easy without at least trying to find them.

As I walk quickly around the free-weights area, my eyes straining in the dark, it occurs to me that only two people knew I'd be here—Stephen and Barnard.

Did those assholes sneak in to watch me and Lexi?

I wouldn't put it past those perverted motherfuckers.

Circling the sparring arena, I turn my head left and right, still searching.

But I know it's futile. I know that, if anyone is in here, I won't find them that easily.

And I'm almost sure it had to be one of my best friends.

Then again, I left the back door open for Lexi and didn't lock it after she walked in.

Shit, shit, shit.

I'm a fucking moron.

I need to get her out of here.

When I head back into the office, she's still sitting on the couch, looking confused.

Adorable.

Her hands are palm-up on her lap and I see they're still covered in my come.

Sexy.

Her eyes meet mine and I reach back to yank my t-shirt over my head. Her eyes widen, pupils snapping wide, eating up every inch of my upper body.

My dick twitches toward her. Kneeling before her, I grab her hands and start cleaning them up with my shirt.

Her cheeks go pink.

My heart beats loud and hard through my body, demanding *her, her, her!* The chant is almost too loud for me to ignore.

"Andrew, your shirt."

"It's okay, baby. I have another in the car." I finish cleaning her up and bring her to her feet. Blood rushes hot and thick through my veins. I want more of her body. Her kisses. Her touch.

More time with her.

It feels like so much of it has already been wasted, even though we're just eighteen.

"Lexi . . ." I swallow thickly. "Would you consider spending the rest of your birthday with me? I want to show my girl a good time."

That blush deepens and I have to bite back a groan. "Andrew, Kaylee is your girlfriend. Not me."

"No," I snap, a little harsher than I should. "You're my girl. The one I've always wanted." The one I love. Cupping her chin, I hold her in place and bring my phone out of my shorts pocket. "As a matter of fact, I'm letting her know. Now."

Lexi watches me as I bring up Kaylee's number and start typing out a text.

Drew: It's over. I'm done. Not doing this anymore. Don't feel you. I'm feeling someone else.

It's harsh, and I'm a major dick for doing it over text, but whatever.

My girl watches me as I hit send. Then, I turn off my phone, because I don't want Kaylee or anyone trying to contact me while I'm focused on Lexi.

"I'm your man. You're my girl. Get me, baby?"

She nods, eyes sparkling.

Holy hell, can my heart calm the fuck down?

"Now, you down to ditch your friends so I can take you to do something fun?"

Biting her lips and smiling, Lexi gives me another nod.

I'm so high on her right now, triumph running through my veins. Finally. *Her.* The girl I've wanted for years. *Mine.*

I'll never let her go. Not now.

I smile at her, feeling how wide that smile is, knowing she can see I'm pathetically ecstatic. "Alright. Come on. Let's get you out of here. There's something I've been dying to show you."

stephen

I can't believe it! That sneaky fucker. I knew he was lying about why he wanted to use uncle Luther's gym.

I knew it had to be about a girl, but fuck. Lexi Berkman. The hottest piece of ass in our school. Hottest tits, mouth. Shit, I'll bet she has a hot pussy, too.

Andrew let me have fun with Kaylee once when they broke up, and didn't care.

I contemplate asking him to let me have a piece of Lexi once he's through with her.

Bullshit. He won't. Motherfucker wants her for himself. I saw that.

Nah. He can't have her. I deserve that ass, not him. I'm going to have her.

I always get what I want. My father taught me that.

"Holy shit!" Barnard hisses as we exit the gym.

Andrew and Lexi left a minute earlier in their separate cars, but I know they're going somewhere together. Because he wants to show "his girl" a good time.

Disgusting. Pussy-whipped already.

I smirk, thinking of the video on my phone. I can use this to my advantage. I know this. Just have to figure out the best way how.

My phone goes off. As soon as I see the name, I'm presented with the opportunity.

Fucking perfect.

Still smirking, I answer. "Hey Kaylee."

"Stephen, where the fuck is Andrew? Is he with you?" she

screeches into the phone. *"He just fucking broke up with me over text!"*

My smirk spreads into a wide smile. So perfect. "I know where he was, and with who. She's the reason he's breaking up with you. How fast can you meet up to talk?"

chapter 16

andrew
present

My hand trembles, sweating as I press it into the handprint scanner. It's sweating too much. The scan fails.

My frustrated growl echoes down the hall. Eyeing the doors, I contemplate wrenching them open. The way I feel right now, I'll rip them apart. Shred right through the steel and titanium.

She's there. On the other side of those doors.

My girl.

My obsession.

The only fucking reason I've survived this long.

I swear to God, if the stupid scanner doesn't read my print this time . . .

It does.

I bend at the waist long enough to let it read my eye, promising myself to get rid of the scanner immediately. Nothing will stand between Lexi and I. Never again.

The software division is on the other side of the doors. Maybe a hundred computer stations. Even more employees.

"Berkman's office!" I bark out, loud enough that my voice echoes throughout the entire space.

No one answers. They all continue to stare at me, in shock. Many of them look scared.

"*NOW!*" I yell.

One girl points a shaking finger at a door toward the back.

I'm there in less than three seconds, practically flying, every limb shaking as the door automatically slides open.

And there she is.

Fuck.

There. She. Is.

That injury that never healed.

That infection that has been festering in my soul for almost a decade.

The wound that I pray never leaves me, even if the disease keeps on spreading.

Her.

Everything.

Her back faces me. Her body is different. More womanly, yet tighter at the same time. She's wearing a black, knee-length dress and her hair's straight, held back in a long pony tail.

I'm immediately hit with a pang at the loss of her curls.

Even with the differences, my soul recognizes her, detonating a ruthless energy in my system.

I can't breathe, shaking like a fucking leaf.

I'm lightheaded, and yet so focused. Nothing else exists. All I see is her.

She finally turns.

Black, large glasses. Different yet so similar.

Those eyes.

God. I clench my fists, my jaw. I clench everything because I'm sure my legs are about to give out on me.

I waited years for this moment. Planned it. Mapped out what I would say. What I would do. How she'd react.

All for nothing. This isn't how I imagined it. She wasn't supposed to be glaring at me like that, pouty lips turned down in a frown.

She's staring at me like . . .

She hates me.

I still love her. Every bit of her. More than before. More than I thought. More than I even imagined.

That hard, bitter expression on her face eases up for a second while her eyes rake me.

Analyzing.

For a moment, I lie to myself, telling myself that deep beyond the loathing I see, there's a small glimpse of the hunger she once felt for me.

But when she looks back at my eyes, all I see is that hate.

Lie or not, I go hard for her. Painfully so. I'm a wreck. Destroyed. Stripped down to the core of my psyche—ground zero of the annihilation she left behind.

Lexi's brow scrunches, her expression morphing to confusion. Like she's studying my reaction. Like it's the last thing she expected.

How could it be? How can she be surprised? I know we only had one night together, but didn't I show her back then how much she meant to me?

I'm so hungry for her. I want to *consume* her. I want her to fill the fucking gaping hole she left in me.

Her lips part and her voice, cold, impersonal, finally acknowledges me. "Mr. Drevlow."

I nearly fall to my knees. That voice. Waited so long to hear it again. My breath hitches—then it's gone. One word leaves my mouth. One rough, desperate word.

"*Lexi*."

chapter 17

lexi
present

a lot can happen in one year. A lot of twisted, fucked-up shit.
And if a lot of that can happen in a year, imagine just how much more can happen in seven.

I thought I got away from the darkness once. That an escape and a new life were finally within my grasp.

In that place of fragile, hopeful naïvety, I made the mistake of trusting the wrong person.

I was alone.

Heartbroken.

Destroyed by the loss of a guy I'd adored.

Stephen took advantage of that. Lured me in. Offered me friendship at a time when I'd needed it the most.

But he doesn't want to be my friend. He wants to *own* me.

Because he "loves" me.

Him. Someone that's too sick to even truly understand the concept of love.

I understand it, but only because of the very woman who he hurt to get at me—my mother. We're all we have. Our connection gives us reason.

Me, a reason to keep going.

Her, a reason to continue fighting for her life.

Thanks to Stephen, she's sick. Lying in a hospital bed, as she has for the last three-and-a-half-years.

He wanted me as part of his company.

He *demanded* that I remain a part of his life.

After he raped me, I refused to do neither.

That's when he went after my mother, infecting her with an aggressive strain of human immunodeficiency virus.

Yes. That son of a bitch infected my mother with AIDS. Not just any kind. We could've gotten help from her health insurance, could've afforded treatment for it on our own. The strain he infected my mother with is a lab created version, one the CDC doesn't even know about yet.

An engineered, super-Hulk version of the virus that would've ended my mother's life in months.

I'm an idiot. I should've never trusted a man that was once *Andrew Drevlow's* best friend. Like attracts like.

They're not friends anymore. As a matter of fact, Stephen despises Andrew.

Hopefully, now that I'm here, I can find out why. Use that to my advantage.

That's who I am now. I don't care for anyone outside of my mother. I don't feel anything except the burning need for revenge.

Stephen was the only one with enough resources to keep my mother alive. I'd had no choice but to enter into that contract and work with his company. Let him take advantage of me again.

It was a lesson hard-learned.

A lesson learned well.

A lesson I thought I had down pat.

Then Richard Drevlow came along, with a promise to get me out from under Stephen's control. With the means to do so and the means to actually help my mother.

Ronald Drevlow's brother.

The man responsible for ruining my father's life and driving him to suicide.

Andrew Drevlow's uncle.

The boy I once loved—was *obsessed* with—and the boy I'd wanted to give myself to more than anything.

The same boy that tricked me, lied to me.

The only man to ever break my heart.

I'm only here to use him. For what he and his uncle can do for me, in return for what I can give them. I'm not here for anything else. Stephen confessed to me once, while drunk, that Andrew *lives* for me. That he never got over me. That he suffers every single waking moment because of me.

I didn't believe it then. I don't believe it now. And none of that matters, I tell myself. I'm not here to see if any of that is true.

But then, a roar echoes into my new office, an inhuman, hair-raising sound.

"Berkman's office!"

My heart . . . *stops*? Oh God, what the hell?

"*NOW!*"

Fear races into my veins, chilling me, slapping me with a brutal, unforgiving truth.

I lied to myself.

I *am* here to see if it's true.

I do care.

There's an echo of Andrew Drevlow still etched into my soul, and I'm here to make damn sure I'm still etched into his.

chapter 18

lexi
present

denial.

We tend to make it our best friend, our constant shields. A perceived strength; a merciless weakness.

Because, in the face of truth, it flees, abandoning you when you need it most.

He's coming.

I can feel the energy that is him—an energy I was once addicted to, a rush I could never truly forget, and it's barreling toward me.

In front of me is a long, metallic shelf that's built into the wall. I went through the trouble of setting up my things on it; my gadgets, a few pictures of my mom.

I'm holding one of those pictures now. Had been staring at it, reminding myself why I agreed to come work here of all places.

It almost falls out of my hand when I hear the pounding footsteps coming closer.

He's . . . he's *running* to me?

The automatic, steel doors slide open, and I have a split second to lower the frame, inhale, try to fucking compose myself.

The running stops.

Even before I register the sound of his rapid breaths, my knees go weak with sensation.

I haven't laid eyes on him yet, and I'm completely breathless.

All those years. All that pain. How were they not powerful enough to erase his effect on me?

Why does it feel stronger than ever, stronger than I even imagined it?

Don't let him see. He can't know. He once used this weakness against me. He thought it'd be funny to play with me, use my feelings for him to lure me in. All so he could seduce me while his friends watched. While they *recorded* the whole thing.

The next day, they showed off that recording. To the entire school.

That old, buried rage and humiliation howl to life inside me. It's a much needed reminder.

My body might be a fool, a victim of a glitching, primal biology, but *I* don't want the man behind me.

I despise him.

I only want what he can do for me.

And every ounce of pain I can rip out of him along the way.

The thought hardens me, pushing back the ludicrous response I'm having to him.

I turn—

And nearly stagger back into the shelf behind me.

It's him. Oh God, it's Andrew Drevlow. I didn't allow myself to keep tabs on him all these years. Didn't look at a single picture.

In many ways, he's still looks the same.

But no, he doesn't. He really, really doesn't.

A *man* stands before me. One that somehow seems taller. Way, way bigger, and he was a tower of muscles at eighteen.

Dressed impeccably in a dark blue suit, he stands there, staring at me, his eyes *eating* me up.

Like he's been starved for the sight of me.

A small place inside me trembles.

His facial expression is so harsh. Everything about him is harsher, harder.

Darker.

A sort of madness glitters in his eyes. It scares me, but only because a part of me awakens for it.

I've been walking around dead for so many years, that part of me gone, eradicated. One look at him and it roars back to life, banging inside me. A volatile storm I'm not sure I can contain.

I hate him. Hate him, I remind myself. And I do. Regardless of everything else I'm feeling, the hate is still there.

But . . . he's shaking.

So am I, can barely hide it. The emotions wrestling within me are too different—disgust. Hate. Rage.

Sadness.

Desire.

Fuck. I still want him?

Looking at him, I know the answer to that loud and clear.

That dark, reddish brown hair.

Those lazy, toffee-colored bedroom eyes.

He was everything I ever wanted once. A mountain of a man I was dying to own.

Now, I can barely stand the sight of him.

His reaction to me is messing with my head. Why does he look like it *burns* him to lay eyes on me? Like all he wants in the world is to come closer?

I swallow, struggling for calm, and finally bring myself to say his name. A name I despise. Another reminder I need. "Mr. Drevlow."

His expressions twists. There's no mistaking the agony in his gaze. The agony I hear when he says my name. "*Lexi.*"

A heart I'd believed to be hardened splits wide open inside my chest. Yearning hits. Hard. Fast.

And then he starts coming at me.

chapter 19

lexi

present

no. Fuck. No.

Heart roaring, I stumble backwards, but there's nowhere to go. My back hits the shelf behind me.

Everything I know, everything I believed the last seven years, every hope I had for my future slams into the floor.

All I have is this moment.

This very second and the horrible truth it brings. The blood rushing in my ears. The speeding of my already bruised heart. The reopening of this chasm within me, a pit of bleak, unforgiving despair I thought I'd closed.

And the very thing my body is pounding for coming at me full-throttle.

He takes my air with his proximity.

My hands slide uselessly along the metal behind me. I don't

know what I'm doing, what I'm looking for.

A way out. I need a—

Andrew grabs me and practically flings me into him.

Suddenly, I'm pressed face-first into his massive chest, his heartbeat like a violent war drum against my forehead.

His scents—it hits.

His arms—they squeeze around me tight.

He trembles. Inhales me.

His cock is a hard, heavy rod against my abdomen.

The world tilts. The core of me shifts.

Hunger pierces me, leaking down my thighs, legs, spreading to every part of me. I lose sensation. My knees buckle.

Andrew catches me up against him, lifting me. His face presses into the crook of my neck. Another inhale. His lips ghost my pulse with his exhale.

I hear the sound of my voice breaking on a whimper.

He melts around me, arms locking with all the strength of his body. A primal groan rumbles out of him—part pain, part hunger, all desperation.

It shouldn't send a pulse of heat through my body.

But it does.

It's strong. Too strong.

I have no choice but to hang onto him.

His chest expands, shoulders rising, a constant growl reverberating within him. His body is coiled.

Like an animal about to strike.

He does.

His teeth snap down around the sensitive skin of my neck.

He bit me!

Andrew doesn't let me go. The tip of his tongue circles the skin trapped between his teeth. Somehow, his arms squeeze harder.

He bites lower, licks me again.

And I do the one thing I would've never thought I'd do; I moan his name. *His nickname.* "*Drew.*"

Andrew groans, pushing forward, pressing me into the shelf behind me. He lets my neck go, rising his head, and I shudder at his expression.

He looks like he's been hit and the pain of that hit is killing him. His large, hot hand encircles the back of my neck, trapping me. His eyes drop to my mouth. That madness again. There's something very, very wrong with him.

This isn't the same Andrew I once knew.

And I want this version more than I ever wanted the other. I want the darkness I sense in him. It thrills me. I'm so wet for it.

After everything I've been through. How could I want that?

Oh God. I'm the sick one!

I place my hands on his shoulders to push him away. He forces his large body between my legs. "Need . . . that mouth, Lexi."

What seems to be a sonic wave of pure energy pounds through my lower body at the thought of him kissing me. Common sense gone, I whisper desperately, "I'll come. I'm going to come if you kiss me."

He groans sharply, eyes flashing, and he dips his head.

Last second, I somehow manage to tilt my head back, avoiding his lips.

If they touch mine, they'll ruin me. Fucking *ruin* me.

Running on pure self-preservation, I push him away, putting all my force into it. I rush away from the shelf, stumbling toward my desk.

The sliding door to my office opens. Richard Drevlow steps through.

I fall into my chair, shaking like an epileptic.

Andrew steps toward me.

Lips pressed together, I shake my head, fighting to hold back the whimpers that want to break through.

"What's going on here?" Richard asks.

I can't formulate a response, trapped by this destructive hunger. Stuck in a memory I've tried so hard to erase—the last time I had Andrew's lips on me, his tongue between my legs.

chapter 20

lexi

7 years ago

i park next to Drew's car in the parking lot. My hands are still shaking. I can't stop replaying what happened back on that couch.

It felt so good.

He felt so good.

I squeeze down on the steering wheel, my thighs rubbing together restlessly.

Drew exits his car and walks around to my side. I'm unable to stop myself from eating up the sight of him as he saunters closer.

His wide shoulders swing back and forth with each step he takes. He changed into a black t-shirt that clearly shows off his tight midsection.

His other shirt is somewhere in his car. Because he used it to clean up my hands after he came all over them.

My cheeks heat up at the reminder.

Hunger gnaws at me.

My slick pussy aches for him.

Drew reaches me. Leaning down, he taps on my window, signaling for me to lower it.

I do so, shaking at his nearness.

"You okay, baby?" he asks with that deep, sexy voice of his.

I remember him moaning for me, the things he said.

His voice breaking on a roar as come spurted out of him and onto my hand.

My lips part. Only one word leaves my mouth. "Drew."

His toffee-colored eyes flash, and his hand reaches into the car, unlocking the door. He yanks it open.

He leans into the car faster than I can process and brings me to his lips.

I moan at the feel of them, wet and thick, owning my mouth completely.

He slides his tongue into me, groaning in the back of his throat.

Nothing has ever tasted as good as Andrew Drevlow.

Nothing has ever smelled as good. Felt as good.

I know that nothing ever will.

He lifts his large hand, running his fingers down my cheek while sucking on my bottom lip.

The hot ache inside me explodes into that familiar, uncontrollable force—a hurricane of pure want, hellbent on ruining me if I don't have him.

"God, those lips." He bites me, ripping a wild groan out of me. "You have no idea, Lexi . . . no idea . . ." His tongue licks mine. "I'll do anything. To anyone."

What is he talking about?

There isn't enough brain power for me to contemplate it. His hand circles the back of my neck and his kiss turns rougher, his body pushing me into the seat.

My body short circuits. I hear my needy whimper above the rush of blood in my ears. I hold onto the back of his head, arching against the seatbelt.

Drew shoots back, accidentally hitting the steering wheel. The blare of the horn makes us jump.

I tremble all the way to the tips of my toes, my hands aching to pull him back to me.

He's breathing like he just ran several miles. The sound turns me on, because I love being the one that turns *him* on.

He moves back to sit on his haunches before me, eyeing me with darkened eyes.

I grab onto the steering wheel again since I have nothing else to grab onto.

"You okay?" he asks again, but his smirk tells me he knows the answer to that very well.

I respond to him honestly. "I can't breathe."

His expression softens into something that steals the last of my breath. "Good. Because I can't either."

Emotion suffocates me. For so many years, I missed him, my once close friend. How could I have forged such an intense connection with him when we'd been only kids?

A better question: how did that connection survive us being separated after what his father did?

Mr. Drevlow drove my father to suicide.

And, yet, I'm connected to his son on a molecular level that frightens me because I know what it means. I knew what it meant the day he approached me and first spoke to me after all those years of not speaking to each other.

"Wait for me here, okay baby? I'm going to get some things for us." Drew motions with his head to the convenience store in front of us.

I nod.

Closing my door, he rises and walks into the store with that lazy, confident swagger.

I want that boy.

He's going to be my first.

Swallowing, I admit the truth to myself.

I'm in love with him and I can't freaking wait to give him my virginity.

chapter 21

lexi
7 years ago

"my boy said it's okay for you to leave your car here. It'll be safe," Drew tells me once he returns. He's holding two shopping bags in his hands. I'm curious as to what's inside them, but don't have a chance to ask him.

Drew reaches through the open window and unlocks my car again.

I have no idea what he has planned for us—for me. Doesn't matter. When he murmurs to me in that rumbly, silky voice, "Turn off the car and get out here, baby," I move faster than I've ever moved in my life.

Every inch of me is shaking as I exit the car, my legs almost too weak to hold me up. "Where are we going?" I ask him, biting my lip in an effort to control my nerves.

I want.

I want so much right now. Too hard. I'm hopeful. Scared. Excited.

I want him to tell me he's taking me somewhere private, really private, where we can be all alone so he can make me his.

Where *I* can make him mine.

Only mine.

I think about Kaylee and all the other girls at school he's probably slept with, and my body flushes with anger.

Then I remember his dick pumping in my hand, how beautiful he looked coming, and greed floods my veins like an unrelenting tidal wave.

"First, you and those sexy lips are coming here." He wraps his free hand around my waist and brings me in.

I go willingly, wrapping my arms around his neck. Our lips meet on a wet slide.

He growls for me, low and hungry.

I moan, utterly desperate.

His tongue forces my mouth open and takes mine, tangling wetly. Pleasure spikes low in my belly. He squeezes my ass, ripping a whimper out of me.

He sucks the air right out of me, and I don't care. My ribs are on fire from the need to breathe, but I kiss him harder. Press closer. Rub my aching body against him.

"Whoa, baby." Groaning, Drew ends our kiss, his panting breaths hitting my wet lips.

My pussy clenches. My frantic fingers move along the back of his head, my hands curling to pull him to me.

His hand tightens on my ass and he licks my jaw. "Yeah, baby, I fucking need you, too." He rocks his hips into me, blatantly rubbing his dick against my lower abs. "But not here." Grabbing my hand, he begins leading me toward his car.

"How about when we get to wherever we're going?" I ask

breathlessly.

Drew presses on the button to unlock his car and the lights flash. He opens the back and carefully places the bags inside. I hear what sounds like glass bottles clinking together. He closes the door and leads me round the side of the car to the passenger side.

I'm very aware he hasn't answered my question, so I tug on his hand. "Drew?"

We make it to the passenger side before he seems to snap. Whirling around, he grabs me and presses me into the sleek, carbon gray surface of his car. His hands sift through my hair, fisting, pulling. Holding onto it like he was dying to grab it.

I get a kiss, one quick, hard kiss, and a low, rough warning. "Don't tempt me, Lexi. I'm trying to do right by you."

My hands slide up his abs, feeling each hard indentation, up, up, until both of his pecs are pressed to my palms.

There's no common sense left in me, no other urge I care to focus on. I want to tempt him. More than anything.

So I do. I arch against the car, letting him feel my needy body on his, and beg him in a soft voice, "Kiss me, Drew. Please."

"So fucking sweet," he groans, giving me what I asked for, what I want. His lips, perfect, firm, owning mine. His tongue slick and unrelenting. Fucking mine.

And it's not enough. Not enough. I need more. I have to be closer. I want him inside me, under my freaking skin if possible.

I need him so damn much that it fucking *hurts*, and I have to suck back a sob at the pounding agony.

Drew lifts me up with one arm around my waist and opens the passenger door. He places me inside and snaps the seatbelt around me as I struggle to catch my breath.

"Drew!" I'm giggling like an idiot, lightheaded with happiness.

"Shush, baby. Let me take you where I want to take you and then I'll take care of you."

I shiver at his words, knowing what they mean now.

He just smirks at me mischievously before heading to his side of the car.

chapter 22

lexi

present

"What's going on here?" Richard Drevlow, while seemingly not as cold and ruthless as his brother had been, is clearly not a man that likes to repeat himself.

I keep my eyes glued to him because looking at his nephew means certain death for me.

Even without looking at him, there's no way I can escape the force of his stare.

"Leave us," Andrew tells his uncle.

Clearly, dominance is a trait that runs in the family.

Andrew's uncle actually seems to contemplate that request.

Silently, my gut tight with dread, I shake my head and beg him with my eyes to stay.

I underestimated that echo. In fact, it's not an echo at all. It's an all-out shriek in my system, this savage, unyielding force rushing hot through my veins.

Andrew's mere presence flooded my mind, scratching at dead pieces of me, unearthing a part of me I'd believed long dead.

I lost the ability to lust after any man the day I ran from him. All I had for so long were the memories of him, that inexorable hold they had on me.

Then Stephen raped me and I lost all contact with the feminine side of my sexuality. It took me years to work past it enough to try having sex with anyone.

And when I finally decided to give Paul a chance, I did it for just that: to try. I felt nothing. No interest. No arousal.

Nothing. Absolutely nothing.

Until a few seconds ago.

"Andrew, I need to speak with you for a moment." Richard hasn't looked away from me.

"No." One word. No room for arguments.

Hands shaking, I straighten in my seat—a false show of resolve. I'm not resolved in any way. I'm ridiculously weak. "I need to get back to work if I'm going to finish the breakdown for the software prototype on time."

"No, Lexi. We're going to talk." Andrew walks to me.

I bite down on the urge to bolt from my seat. "You're already over budget and behind schedule—"

"Lexi, *please*."

There's raw, unfiltered desperation in his tone. The kind that can't be faked.

I remember Stephen, drunk, belligerent, laughing bitterly. I remember his claim that, in the end, the thing that destroyed Andrew the most was *me*.

I didn't believe that, either.

Refuse to believe it now.

I *can't* believe it. Just can't.

Oh God, this isn't how this was supposed to go.

"Mr. Drevlow," I address Richard, fighting for calm. "I would like to be left alone so that I can work on the coding." Please, please, get your nephew out of here . . .

Andrew slams his hand on my desk. I jump with a gasp. "I don't give a fuck about the coding!" That bellow, as loud as his scream was when he demanded to know where my office is, makes my head snap around.

Toffee-colored eyes, framed by those heavy, heavy lashes.

Hunger.

Insanity.

A pain so deep that it almost makes a mockery of my own.

"I waited seven years for you." His voice breaks, his chest heaving with each breath. "You were all that mattered. You were all that kept me fucking going." His eyes search mine, and I struggle not to cry. "Talk. To. Me."

His uncle tries to get his attention. "Andrew."

Andrew doesn't acknowledge him.

I can't . . . I can't function under that look. If I believe what he says . . . *no, Lexi.* This man conspired with his friends to ruin me. Just like his father once ruined mine.

Andrew *admitted* to the school board that he was in on the plan along with his fucking girlfriend Kaylee and his two best friends, Stephen and Barnard. They were all kicked out of the school mere days before graduation for what they did to me.

Maybe this is remorse. Unadulterated guilt. A guilt he's lived with for almost a decade.

The thought infuriates me. "Mr. Drevlow, you either walk out of this office right now and leave me to do my work," my voice shakes with anger," or I'll walk out of this building and disappear. And don't doubt that I can."

I'm bluffing. My mom is stuck in that hospital and I no longer have Stephen to help keep me hidden. *Please, don't realize this.*

Andrew's eyes bounce all over my face, landing on my mouth, growing darker, locking with my eyes again—

His hand snaps around the back of my neck. "Fine, but not before I remind you of something," he growls.

His hot skin on mine. That growl. The violent greed in his stare.

Another gasp leaves me—a needy exhale.

Groaning, Andrew pulls me to him and fits his lips over my own.

chapter 23

lexi

7 years ago

after driving for about twenty minutes, Drew pulls off onto the side of the road. On our left, across the road, is nothing but thick woods.

On our right, it's all open field, as far as the eye can see. And above that? Stars. Nothing but stars.

It's breathtaking.

Drew turns off the ignition. I turn away from the view outside. He's watching me in the dark, his face highlighted by the headlights.

My throat tightens at the way he stares at me. He's completely focused, barely blinking. His eyes bore into mine.

I remember that look. He gave it to me when I kissed the corner of his mouth.

Right before he devoured my own.

"Drew?" My tone is low. Hungry.

God, how can I convince him to take me right here?

He pops his jaw, shifting restlessly in his seat. His hand reaches for mine, but he pulls back at the last second, curling it into a fist. "Come." He exits the car in a hurry.

I follow him, disappointed. He gets the bags out of the back and opens the trunk to remove what seems to be a folded blanket. I stand here, watching him the whole time, hands tightly intertwined because all I want to do is reach out to him.

And I can't.

I don't have the guts to do so. Don't know why, but he seems closed off right now, and I don't know how to approach him.

Drew comes around the side toward me. "Let's go." He motions with his head at the open field.

"Let me help you with that." I reach my hand out to help him with one of the bags.

The corner of his mouth tilts up in a tender smile. "Here, baby. Just carry this." He holds out the folded blanket.

Smiling at him, I take it, then follow him onto the grass. We don't go far. Drew left the headlights on, and I suspect he wants us close enough to their glow.

He stops. Placing the bags on the ground, he takes the blanket and spreads it out for us.

We sit together and he reaches into the bags. First, he brings out one of those cheese and crackers party platters. Next, it's two bottles of wine, one red and one white. He gives me a rueful smile as he reaches for two clear plastic cups. "If it was up to me, we'd be sitting in a really nice place, drinking out of real glasses."

I shake my head, my heart in my throat. "This is perfect." It's impromptu, but no one has ever done anything this sweet for me before. "Thank you so much, Drew."

He pauses in the middle of uncorking one of the bottles, eyeing me with that expression that makes me ache in my chest.

Between my legs.

Christ, my brain's hurting as I stare at him.

"Lexi, baby. This is nothing. I plan to give you everything."

"Oh, God. Drew. I—" *I love you. I love you so damn much and I need you to feel the same way. Because if you don't, it's going to break me.*

Drew leans toward me, pinning me with his gaze. "You what, Lexi?" There's an urgency in his quiet tone, an inexorable demand.

He wants my answer and he wants it to be nothing but the truth.

I can't give him that. I'm too afraid. "I'm just . . . I'm just really grateful."

Expression soft, he leans over and kisses my cheek.

Exhaling roughly, I turn my head. The corner of my mouth skims along the corner of his. I don't try to move away, but Drew fists my hair regardless, forcing me to stay where I am.

Just like at the gym.

My lips part with a whimper.

Groaning, he tilts his head, letting our lips skim each other.

A whisper of a touch.

Nothing but a tease.

I mouth his name against his lips, my chest racing too fast to form coherent words.

"*Lexi.*" He drags his teeth across my bottom lip, sucks on it a little, hungry sounds echoing in the back of his throat.

Shaking, I open my mouth to tell him that I want him to take me. I want him to be my first, and I want it to happen *now*.

He makes a strained noise, what sounds almost like a broken "no" and puts distance between us. His hands tremble as he uncorks the wine bottle and opens the cheese and crackers tray.

I swallow another round of disappointment—until Drew hands me a cup and says, "You see those stars up there? I've been thinking of showing you this view for a long time, baby. As long as I've been dreaming of making you my girl. So let's take it easy for a bit, 'K?"

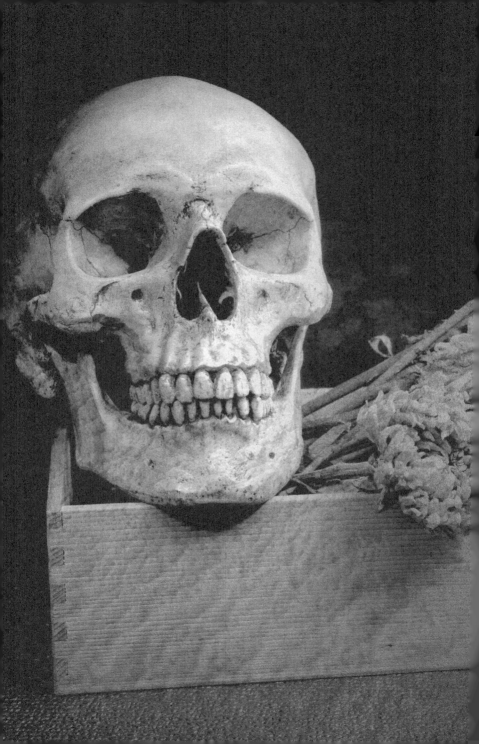

chapter 24

lexi

7 years ago

i haven't fully caught my breath since I walked into the office of that gym and saw Drew's facial expression.

And he just keeps on taking my breath away, over and over.

Emotion clogs my throat, all the things I feel for him fighting to make themselves known. I nod at him instead of speaking, fear a tight band around my chest.

I love him. I love him too much, but I can't tell him that yet.

Drew's lips stretch into a devastating smile. "That's my girl."

I'm going to explode. No way my body can contain this much emotion.

He holds out the cheese tray to me. I take it with my free hand while he pours himself some wine.

"I've never drunk before," I confess.

He places the bottle on the grass besides the blanket and leans back on his elbow. His toffee-colored eyes twinkle with amusement. "You've never had any type of alcohol before?"

I shake my head.

His smile is full of disbelief. "At all?"

Holding back a smile, I shake my head again. "Don't make fun of me." My face heats up and I'm grateful I'm facing opposite the car's headlights. I'm inexperienced in every way, nothing like the girls he's used to.

The last thing I want is him seeing me blush like some innocent little girl.

That sexy smile on his face turns tender, like he finds it adorable that I've never had a drink before, and I can't help but bristle.

Without thinking about it, I decide to throw back a mouthful of wine.

It's dry. Like, really, really dry, and I'm unprepared. Clapping my lips shut, I try not to cough, or let the tears building in my eyes leak out. Eyeliner trails aren't cute.

Drew tugs lightly on my earlobe. "Easy, baby. Especially the first time."

A small cough escapes and I glare at him. "I'm not sure I like this one. It's"—I cough again and cover my mouth before continuing—"really dry."

"Sorry." He takes the cup from me and hurries to pour me some white wine instead. "Here. Just a little. Try it. Slowly."

I raise the cup to my lips, careful not to chug it back this time.

Drew watches my mouth as I tentatively take another sip, the intensity in his eyes almost frightening.

I barely taste the wine. My lungs feel like they're going to burst from lack of oxygen. Even so, I can't stop staring at him while he stares hungrily at my mouth.

"Does that one taste better?" he asks, voice gruff.

"I don't know," I whisper back, not caring about the wine one bit. What I really want is to taste his lips again.

"Have another taste, then."

Oh God, that tone. It's getting lower, rougher, almost dangerous. I clench my thighs together and lift the cup to my lips again. Somehow, I manage to take my time, hold the wine in my mouth long enough to actually process it.

He watches like it's the most interesting thing he's ever seen— like he'd rather be watching nothing but *me*.

He makes me nervous and I'm only drinking wine!

"So?" His eyebrows rise, but his eyes don't move one bit. The way he stares at my lips fills me with wanting.

I don't think I'm going to be able to restrain myself much longer; I want to kiss him again so badly. Staring at his lips, I lick my own, wondering how he'll react if I just grab his face and kiss him.

"Baby?"

Fuck, I shiver every time he calls me that. He makes me feel absolutely crazy. "It's good . . . sweeter."

"Good." He gives me his cocky, happy smile, pleased at himself for picking out a wine I like. "Now we're going to catch up."

The buzz in my veins grows stronger, morphing from excitement to anxiety. I don't know why. Maybe because my life isn't anywhere near as interesting as his is.

I rather speak about what goes on in his life rather than what goes on in mine.

I shift nervously. "What do you mean catch up?" He won't stop watching me. Is he even blinking?

"I want to know everything, Lexi. Everything you've been up to these last eight years."

My heart beats harder. Talking to him about this makes me uncomfortable.

And then he asks me the one question I really don't want to answer.

The one question sure to bring up the darkness that stands between us.

"How's your mom doing?"

chapter 25

lexi
7 years ago

drew's father once worked with my father. To be more exact, my father was hired to work at Drevlow Systems, Inc., thirteen years ago.

A huge achievement. Just what we needed at the time to give us a better life.

The pay would also allow him to work less hours, have more time to develop his prototype.

And he did. 'Til this day, I have no idea what he built, but it was his life's dream. The thing he wanted most out of life.

Ronald Drevlow found out about it, decided he wanted the prototype so he could make money off it. My father refused. It was *his* invention.

No one refuses Ronald Drevlow anything. Over a period of three years, he systematically terrorized my father, broke our lives apart bit by bit, until there was nothing left.

My father had no choice but to sell the prototype to Mr. Drevlow.

My mother didn't find out about it until shortly after my father's death.

He killed himself and left us every dollar he'd gotten on the sale as part of our inheritance.

I was ten-years-old. That same week, my mother urged me to stop speaking to my best friend, the son of the man that ruined our lives.

Of course, I refused.

That is, until I realized that Drew had distanced himself from me.

He hadn't died like my father did, but losing him hurt almost as much.

"You don't want to talk about her with me, do you?" There's sadness in Drew's eyes, but also understanding.

It's not his fault what his father did. But I have to ask him the one thing that's been eating at me for almost eight years. "Why did you stop talking to me when your father told you to?" He never let me know that, yet I know his father had something to do with it.

If my mother asked me to stop talking to him, there's no way his father didn't ask the same of him.

Drew runs his hand across the top of his head, back and forth in an agitated manner.

This is a wound between us that neither of us wanted to explore.

He opened the door to this discussion by asking about my mom.

"My father—" He stops abruptly and looks out into the dark field in front of us. "He warned me that if I didn't stop talking to you, he'd go after you and your mom since he was done with your father."

Anger vibrates through him. His lips are tense with strain, and his free hand clenches and unclenches. He throws back the rest of his wine and refills his cup before looking at me. "I was ten, and . . ."

TWISTED HEARTBREAK

I place my hand over his; immediately, he turns his hand and intertwines our fingers. "I get it." I really do. He was just a boy and his father is a scary son of a bitch.

I wish I could say his bark is bigger than his bite, but it's not. The man has no qualms about destroying people.

Drew lowers his wine and cups my face.

I can't control my reaction, and nuzzle his palm, soaking in the feel of his skin.

His eyes plead with me for a forgiveness I've already given him. "Lexi, I was scared out of my fucking mind he'd make good on his threat. And then time passed, and we'd already grown apart, you know."

"I know." I stare at our hands, my heart aching from the memory of those years.

My mom never told me why we stayed in town, why she used the money my father left us to keep me in the same private schools as Drew.

Yeah. Thanks to that inheritance, we're well off.

Not that it changes anything.

Things got hard for us regardless. My father's death altered us in a twisted way. My mother was never the same again.

And I . . . sometimes I don't recognize myself in the anger I keep trapped inside me. It makes me want to do things. Things I know for a fact I shouldn't.

I love Drew, but I'd have no problem ending his father's life if I could.

What type of person does that make me?

"Drew . . ." The fear is back, making it hard to speak. I don't want to voice the question going through my mind, but how could I not? "How are we supposed to make this work between us? Let's be realistic here. I don't think—I . . ." I let go of his hand to cover my face. "We can't."

BOOK ONE

chapter 26

lexi
present

i'm a fool.

I was a fool seven years ago when I convinced myself I could be with Andrew Drevlow of all people.

A fool the day I decided to work for Stephen.

I'm still a fool today, sitting in this damn office.

I'm a fucking idiot who's yearning to kiss Andrew again, even after I jerked back hard enough to send my chair skidding feet away from him.

His chest is racing.

Mine is, too.

He's staring down at me with that challenge in his eyes. Like he knows what I'm struggling with and he's daring me to face it.

Fuck him.

I glare at him with all the loathing I feel.

"Drew . . ." His uncle watches him warily. I'm sure he's realized how insane his nephew is. "I'm going to have to ask you to come with me."

Drew's body coils, a slow tightening of muscle. "You're not the boss here, Uncle Richard. I am. You made sure of that. So I'm going to have to ask *you* to leave." His eyes remain on mine the entire time. What a fucking bastard. "*I* want you to leave. How about that?"

"I'm not going anywhere."

I remember that hard determination. Last time I saw it, he'd stared at me in that dark field, swearing he would never let his father hurt me again—and swearing he would never let me go.

All lies. He hadn't been determined to protect or have me.

He'd been determined to pull off the prank he and his friends had come up with.

"If you don't leave my office, Mr. Drevlow, I will get up and walk out of this building right now."

"You're under contract, you can't."

I grind my teeth together. "I did it with Menahan. Watch. Me."

"I'm nothing like Stephen," Andrew enunciates slowly.

"Oh, really? What do you call grabbing me against my will and kissing me?" I realize way too late what I've just said.

His eyes go dark. Absolutely black within the span of a second. Fast enough to warn me.

Scare me.

This isn't the same Andrew I knew years ago. This is a madman. A possibly deranged man that's ready to harm somebody.

"What did he do to you?" His tone sends a cold shiver through me.

"Nothing!" My heart is beating painfully and I'm trembling.

I'm scared. So scared of what I see in Andrew's expression.

This man is capable of murder. Every instinct in my body screams it at me.

"Lexi, I will not ask you again."

TWISTED HEARTBREAK

"And I will not ask you, Mr. Drevlow. Please leave me to my work or I'll leave." I can't look at him. His eyes are drilling me, and if I don't look away, he's going to rip every secret out of me.

Maybe I should let him. I should tell him everything and let him ruin his life by hurting Stephen.

But who would help my mother then?

I stand up, restless, trapped by the nervous energy I feel.

Andrew moves closer to me.

I practically leap back. "Sta—stay away from me."

"That's why you want to ruin him, isn't it? He hurt you—WHAT THE FUCK DID HE DO TO YOU, LEXI?"

I slap my hands over my ears at that roar.

Stephen lied to me.

Tricked me.

Raped me.

Infected my mother.

Kept me prisoner under his control for years.

Eventually, he raped me again.

Andrew is obsessed with getting an answer.

Possibly obsessed with me.

Oh God, he *is* like Stephen. Both of them want to own me even though they've both hurt me.

What Andrew did was despicable; what Stephen did, all of it, falls under the definition of heinous.

I have to pick one devil to battle another, and in order to win, I have to keep the truth from one of them. Shaking, I cross my arms and face Andrew.

A monster's fury stares back at me.

"I'll—I'll tell you." Not the whole truth. Never that. But enough to placate him. "But you have to leave this office *now*."

"Lexi."

"Leave now, or I will!"

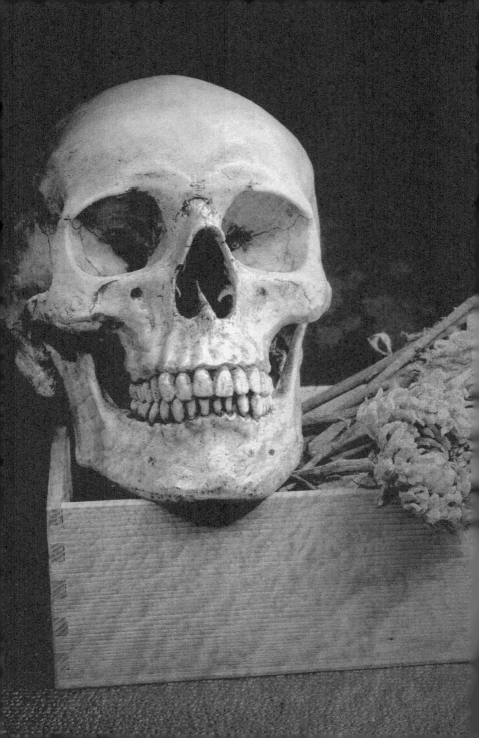

chapter 27

<u>lexi</u>
7 years ago

"i don't blame you for thinking that." Drew places the blanket back in his trunk. The bag with the leftover food and wine goes next.

I'm so stupid. I fucked it up. He barely spoke after I muttered that dumb sentence, and now he's cutting our date short. Just because I had to open my big fucking mouth.

It's a logical thought. Us being together is an impossibility. A chasm full of obstacles stands between us.

I don't care. Right now, it feels like he's shutting down on me, listening to the logic behind my statement. Distancing himself.

A taste. That's what tonight has been. And it's not enough. I'll never have enough. I need more of Drew. So much more. I can't lose him. Not yet. Maybe not ever.

Definitely not tonight.

He comes to me, placing his hand on the small of my back, leading me to the passenger side. "I've thought about it, Lexi. I don't even have the power to protect you from my asshat of a father." Staring off into space, he opens the door for me. "I don't have the power. Not yet."

My body freezes over as he turns to walk to the driver's side.

I can't let him shut down on me. Can't let him walk away.

He's walking around his car by the time I snap out of it. "Drew!" I run to him.

He jerks to a stop, turning in surprise.

I jump up into his arms. "I don't care. I don't care, Drew."

Drew groans my name, hugging me tight. "Lexi, you're right. He can hurt you. He *will*. I knew this when I decided to come after you."

"I don't care, Drew. I just want you. So bad."

Another groan. He grabs my hair, nuzzling my face roughly. He's hard again, throbbing against me. *Calling* me.

"I want you, Drew. Please. Take me. Make me yours. I don't want to belong to anyone else."

"Fuck, baby." Yanking me back, he stares into my eyes.

Panting, I try to bring him closer, knowing that my eyes are pleading with him.

"God, Lexi. I fucking need you."

"Take me. Take me, Drew."

He exhales slowly, his body tensing more and more. "Baby, I'm losing it here. I can't . . . It's not time, yet. I—I need you too bad."

"*Yes.*"

His lips crash onto mine, roughly. Painfully. His tongue pushes into my mouth, not giving me a choice.

I open for him without hesitation, his tongue a wet slide against my own. It drives me crazy, leaves me clenching and unclenching desperately.

TWISTED HEARTBREAK

Drew clutches my ass, rolling his hips into me. I lift my leg up on his hip, opening myself to more of his thrusts. His cock presses right where I need it. Pleasure zings, and I go lightheaded, almost coming at each slide of his erection along my clit.

"Drew. More, please."

He kisses me again, turning me, leading me backwards. The back of my knees hit the hood of his car. Hands wrapped around my waist, he lifts me up onto the hood, laying me on it. I spread my legs and pull him between them, circling my hips up to meet his.

His teeth sink softly into the side of my chin. "You turn me on so fucking much."

I tilt my head back to give him more access. "Take me."

Moaning, he works his hand between us, his fingers skimming my wet panties. The fingers of his other hand curl into the top of my dress. He already broke the straps back at the gym, so when he pulls on my dress, it slides down without issue.

He wastes no time, lips latching around one nipple, his thumb and forefinger squeezing down around the other.

I cry out into the night, arching, my nipples even more sensitive than the first time he played with them.

Drew thrusts into me in circles. Last time, I rode his thigh, and the pleasure was indescribable. Feeling his hard dick nudging my pussy with each thrust makes me even dizzier. "Drew. Oh God, Drew. More. Faster. *More*."

"Fuck Lexi!" Snarling, he bites the side of my breast, then moves to the other and does the same, his fingers playing with both my nipples. "You get me so fucking riled up. I just wanna come all over you. In you." His fingers find my pussy again, pulling my panties aside. "I want this pussy wrapped tight around me."

I bite down on my lip, mewling, nails digging into the back of his head. "I want it, too, Drew. It hurts. In there. I—" My voice breaks on a scream as one of his fingers slide into me.

"Oh God," he breathes frantically, staring up at me, thick lips parted. "Fuck, baby. *Fuck.*"

"Yours. All—yours—*Drew*," I keen, my body wanting—no, *needing* to be fucked by him. My hips rock back and forth, riding his finger, my body soaking in the pleasure each thrust brings. "Fucking, hell. Look at you." His teeth bare on a growl, his eyes eating me alive. Leaning down, he slowly wraps his lips around my nipple, then sucks hard, his thumb circling my clit languidly.

I scream, coming, coming so fucking hard that I can't breathe, can't see, can't think. The pleasure ripples through my clit, my inner walls, my nipples as he sucks and licks on them.

Drew pulls back, breaths practically wheezing, his eyes wild. "So wet. So luscious. I need that in my mouth, baby. Need to eat you while you come."

chapter 28

lexi

7 years ago

i stare up at the night sky, my vision winking in and out, completely out of breath.

Drew wants to come inside me and it turns me on like crazy.

He crawls down my body. I feel his hands on my knees, drawing my legs up. He parts them. His words register.

Was he talking about kissing me? *There*?

My panties are shoved aside.

"Drew? Drew, wait." I scramble up onto my elbows. The sight of him between my legs stops every single thought in my head.

He's staring at me, at my spread, bared pussy, his expression tight with raw lust. "Holy fuck, Lexi. You're perfect."

I moan.

Drew reaches between my legs, smoothing his thumb over my clit softly.

My nails scrape into the hood of the car. "Oh . . . my . . . God."

He nuzzles my clit with the tip of his nose. "Look at that little clit tremble for me."

I'm choking. This is too intense. Too intimate. He's too close.

His breath ghosts over my sensitive flesh with his next words. "All I want to do is eat you."

I need him to. Why was I even nervous about him doing that to me? Forgetting about everything but how horny he makes me, I lean back and spread my legs wider for him.

"That's it baby." He parts my lips open with his thumb, his touch gentle. "Just lay back. Let me take care of you."

I do as he tells me, but lift up my head to look down at him. No way I'm missing this.

He bites the corner of his lip, eyes flashing with hunger. "Such a pretty pussy." Looking up at me, he lowers his head and gives me a wet, soft kiss.

A fierce shot of pleasure arches my back.

Drew eases away a bit. "Like that, baby?"

I grab onto the back of his head and try to push him back to me. "*More.*"

Smiling, he gives it to me. Another light kiss followed by a quick flick of his tongue.

"Jesus, Drew." I can't believe the intensity of this. The pleasure.

His tongue slides over me again, lazily circling my clit. He hums, tasting me, sucking me into his mouth.

"Baby. Don't stop. Please." My hips rock up to meet every glide of his tongue. The look on his face only makes me burn hotter. Rotating my hips faster, I whisper, "I'm going to come. Can't hold it."

He licks me harder, sucks on my clit, his low growls vibrating through me.

I never knew it could be like this. Pleasure bordering on pain.

TWISTED HEARTBREAK

I should feel ashamed at the indecent way Drew's sucking on my pussy, but the dirtiness of it is too fucking delicious not to love.

I writhe on his tongue, chasing more of that sensation. We're alone on this stretch of road, and it makes me even more uninhibited. Drew strokes me with his lips, his tongue, sliding it down, teasing my opening. "Fuck, Lexi. Your pussy's luscious. I've never tasted anything like it."

A fresh wave of wetness slicks my sex; he laps it up, humming again. "Drew. Your tongue. It's so good."

He smiles against my pussy and the sight of his plump, wet lips rips a cry out of me. "Yeah? You like my tongue, baby?"

I nod breathlessly.

His tongue pierces me.

My body clenches, trying to keep him there. I don't want him to stop. Don't want to let him go. Ever. I need more of this pleasure, want him harder, deeper.

He takes his tongue from me. I groan, feeling like I'm about to go mad. "I feel you throbbing on my tongue."

I bite the inside of my cheek. My tight nipples hurt so bad that I don't stop to think or question my impulse. Reaching up, I pinch them between my fingers. Pleasure rushes straight to my pussy.

Drew watches me throb, then his eyes freeze on my nipples, watching me play with them. "I'll never let anyone hurt you. Especially not my father." He stares into my eyes. "You're mine and I'm never fucking letting you go."

"It's all I want, Drew," I moan, squirming on the hood. "Take me. I *need* to be yours."

"You remember that, baby. Remember how much you need me to own you. When it gets tough. When shit gets impossible. You. Remember. That."

I nod at him. At this point, I'll promise him anything, swear to anything. Whatever he wants. I don't care.

BOOK ONE

Seeming pleased, he licks over my clit—slow, hard pressure. He does it one more time, leaving me shaking. On the brink.

Sweat drips down the side of my face despite the cool breeze. I mumble his name, too weak to do anything else.

He thrusts his tongue back into me.

My mind disintegrates in blistering pleasure. Reality splinters into nothing but pounding, white waves of ecstasy, slamming into me. Drowning me.

I lose touch with reality. When I come to, Drew is easing me up into his arms, hugging me as tight as he can.

As if he's about to die and he can't imagine letting me go.

I wrap my weak arms around him and hang on for dear life.

"I meant it, Lexi," he says roughly. But I already know. I feel the intent pounding off him. "Nothing can make me let you go now."

chapter 29

andrew
present

four hours and thirty-seven minutes. That's how long it's been since Lexi came back into my life. Since I smelled her, tasted the sweet skin of her neck. Felt her heart racing against me.

Since I had those lips on mine once more.

Seven fucking years and that small, quick feel of her lips almost made me come on contact.

She kicked me out of her office, and the only reason I listened was because of the look in her eyes.

Fear.

Despair.

Fucking *trauma*.

I'm not a specialist but only a blind moron wouldn't see the signs. Something fucking happened to my girl. Something that broke her.

What did Stephen do to her?

I resist the urge to slam my fist into my desk, but only because I already cracked the glass surface earlier.

I've been watching her since I left her office. It wasn't hard to hack into the security feed. All three of the monitors on my desk are now focused on her.

I'm surprised Lexi made no move to secure those feeds. Clearly, she never expected me to hack into her office's cameras. She truly has no idea how obsessed with her I am. No clue what she means to me.

My fault. I didn't do enough to show her all those years ago.

Lexi left the same day Kaylee played that screwed-up video in front of the school. That same day, I confessed to the cops. Told them I was in on the plan to humiliate Lexi—*after* I almost killed Stephen outside the building.

He was rushed by ambulance to the nearest hospital. I was dragged straight to jail to answer for the attack. My father was one of the largest donors to the school.

So was Stephen's. They weren't going to go after him on my suspicion alone. I had no choice but to lie. I told them Stephen agreed to record me and Lexi for my personal enjoyment. If I hadn't, they never would have dared go after Menahan's son.

They got a hold of Kaylee's phone and were able to trace the file transfer to Stephen. He'd also shared another copy of the file with Barnard.

We all got thrown out days before graduation. Our parents' wealth was the only thing that kept us from losing our diplomas.

My father was furious.

I didn't give a fuck. Lexi had disappeared by then. She and her mother moved without a trace.

Thanks to my fucking father.

The beginning of my downward spiral. I started drinking almost immediately after.

A fucking huge mistake. On so many levels. I should have gone after Stephen and killed him when I had the chance.

Instead, I became consumed with destroying myself.

And the whole time he'd known where my girl was. Somehow, he convinced her to work for him.

At some point during all that, he hurt her.

My mind twists. Lexi stared at me, frightened, comparing me to Menahan because I kissed her.

Against her will.

Lexi, jumping away from me as I walked closer, shaking like a fucking leaf. Stammering.

Blood pounds in my head from the fury. She reacted like many of the girls I went to rehab with. Girls that grew up in unstable homes. Girls with broken lives, regardless of the fact they came from money.

Victims of abuse.

Victims of . . .

No. I can't think it. I just got her back. I can't afford to go to jail for murder now that I've found her.

He's going to die, but I have to be smarter about it.

Lowering my head, I scrub my face with my hands, then look back at the monitors. Lexi is still typing away at her computer.

As she has been since I left her office. Single-minded focus. A woman on a mission.

She wants to help me succeed so she can hurt Menahan.

"What did he do to you?" I whisper at the monitors, dragging my hands down my face.

Of course, no answers are forth-coming. Not yet. I already have a team on it. All of it. I want any information I can find that pertains to all the years Lexi was gone. And I finally know where to start. Menahan's servers. It won't be easy getting past his security, but I will.

I lean back in my chair, inside my dark office, surrounded by the night skyline on two sides, and I can't look away from Lexi.

Everything I want is in that office, forty-two stories down, and I can't go to her.

She found out what I told the cops. Probably blames me for whatever path her life took the last seven years.

"I still love you, Lexi." I never told her back then. It's not the right time to tell her now.

But, God damn it, I've got to do *something*.

Two hours later, I'm still sitting here, contemplating it, when Lexi gets up to leave for the day.

Not thinking about it, I get up to follow her.

chapter 30

lexi

7 years ago

drew takes me back into town. I expect him to drive us straight to my car. He doesn't. He drives to the park and pulls into the dark lot by the pier.

I turn to face him. He does the same, and we sit here for hours, talking. Drew starts off by telling me what's been going on in his life all these years. It's hard watching him talk about his mom. How much she's suffered thanks to his father.

It's not outright stated, but I can tell he's also suffered thanks to that man. Drew got into kickboxing because he needed an outlet for all the anger his father causes him.

No wonder he got so big the last few years. Between that and football, he's in spectacular shape.

With every new thing he tells me, I hate his father more.

With everything, I get hungrier for him. I missed out on so

much. I want to know all of it.

Eventually, I realize what he's doing. *Tit for tat.* He's opening up first. Showing me he's comfortable giving me all his facts—the good, the bad.

When he goes quiet, I swallow and gather the courage to finally tell him everything.

It's odd talking about my mother, how different she is nowadays. Sad. Withdrawn.

The sympathy on his face doesn't help. His father caused our pain, but I don't want Drew to feel guilty about it. "None of it is your fault."

"I'm his son."

"You can't control his actions."

"Trust me, I know that. But he's my father and I can't help but feel somewhat responsible for all you and your mother have been through."

I think of my mother and how she'll possibly react when I confess to her that I'm talking to Drew again—that I'm *with* him. She won't react as negatively as Drew's father will at the news, but she will be disappointed. I know she will.

It breaks my heart, yet I'm willing to face it.

"Don't make me tell you again, Drew. It's not your fault. I can't imagine how hard it is to be his son." I reach over to place my hand on his cheek.

He nuzzles my palm and my heart squeezes painfully. "You really don't know, Lexi. Sometimes . . . sometimes I really wish he would die."

I gasp.

Staring at me worriedly, he places his hand over mine to keep it on his cheek. "I'm sorry, Lexi, but that's how he makes me feel. I fucking *hate* him for what he did to you, to your family, to my mom. To me." His eyes lose their focus.

I can only imagine what he's thinking about right now. What that monster that fathered him has put him through.

He thinks I'm shocked because of his desire to see his father dead; in reality, I'm stunned that we feel the exact same way.

"Drew, it's okay. I understand."

"You do?" The sad uncertainty in his eyes kills me. Before I can respond, he gives this little laugh and shakes his head. "Of course you do. If anyone has the right to want my father dead, it's you."

I nod, broken inside. For him, not for me. This darkness his father caused in me has become so familiar over the last five years. I fought it at first, ran from it.

The faster I ran, the faster it seemed to come after me. Eventually, I let it catch up with me. Welcomed it. This is who I am now. If I could find a way to get close enough to Drew's father and end his life without getting caught, I would gladly do so.

I'm okay with that.

More than okay. It is my firm belief that the world would be a much better place without Ronald Drevlow in it.

But Drew . . . my poor Drew. He's not used to the darkness. Thoughts of murder are new to him. They scare him. So much.

I caress his cheek, my heart hurting for him. If I could spare him this new facet of himself, I would, but trying to do so means lying to him. Letting him believe I don't understand, when I do.

"It's okay to feel that way," I whisper, still caressing him.

"About my own father, Lexi?" His look of disbelief is kind of adorable.

My lips twitch. God, every second that passes I want this guy more and more. "Baby, you happened to get saddled with a demon of a father. You're human. You're allowed to feel the way you feel."

Drew grabs my hand and laces our fingers together. He has that aroused, sexy look in his eyes. "Call me that again."

I bite my lip, feeling my cheeks heat up. "I didn't even realize I called you that."

"Don't care. Say it again." He leans toward me, eyes getting lazier, locked on my mouth.

I do, whispering, "Baby."

His hand snakes around the back of my head, and then he kisses me, slow, languidly, each lick of his tongue getting me wetter. "God," he groans against my lips, tilting his head and kissing me deeper.

I moan in the back of my throat, blindly reaching for my seatbelt to get it off.

A light bite of my lip, and he moves back, his breaths harsh in the car.

I'm still trying to find the clip of my seatbelt.

One look at his expression stops me.

"I mean it, Lexi. I don't care how wrong it is. I'm killing my father for you."

chapter 31

andrew
7 years ago

i can't get over the look Lexi gave me. After our conversation in my car, I drove her back to pick up hers and followed her home. No way was I going to let her drive back this late on her own.

A few blocks from her house, she parked her car. I pulled up behind her and we stood outside for a good ten minutes, just holding onto each other.

It feels fragile, this thing between us. Like anything could break it apart—tears *us* apart again. Nothing will. I can't imagine losing her again. Nothing can get between us.

Except my father.

Lexi's last words before I left come back to me.

"Please, Drew. If you do anything to him, it'll haunt you for the rest of your life."

"I'm not saying I'm going to do anything tonight," I told her.

"But something has to be done, Lexi. He'll never leave us alone."

"Then let me be the one to do it." Her eyes glittered at me, pleading. Steady. *"When you figure out what you're going to do to get rid of him, let me be the one to handle it."*

So naïve. She was resolved. Comfortable with the idea. Whereas I'm still breaking out into cold sweats thinking about getting rid of my father. I tighten my numb, shaking hands around the steering wheel.

I don't care how comfortable she is with the idea, I'm not letting her get involved in any way. If this backfires, it'll be on me. Only me. Fuck, I don't even have a plan. Not yet anyway. I'll figure something out eventually. I have no choice.

I get home around 2:00am. When I pull into our large, sprawling driveway, I see my father's car pulling into the garage in front of me.

Great. Just who I want to see.

I play with the idea of stopping, dimming my lights, trying to escape his notice.

Too late for that. I bet he already saw my headlights behind him. Bracing myself, I drive into the eleven-car garage behind him. My parking spot is on the far left of the garage, his is on the right. I could try and use this as my chance to escape any sort of confrontation with him.

But hell no, I won't. I'm tempted. No matter what I do, the little boy that once wanted his love is still inside me. Still scared. Cowering.

I'm not a pussy, I remind myself. I'm a man now, a man ready to fight for his woman. A man ready to do whatever is necessary to have her *and* keep her safe.

That starts with facing my father.

"Andrew!" He calls out, coming closer.

I've already stopped next to my car to wait for him, keys clutched tight in my hand. I watch him getting closer and realize he's walking oddly.

Damn it, he's drunk.

This situation just keeps on getting better.

He gets within a few feet of me and I notice that his tie is in his hand. His shirt is partly unbuttoned. There's makeup marks all over his collar.

I think of my mother, how I'm sure she once loved this asshole. The cocky smirk on his face pisses me off. It's a familiar face. And not just because he's my father. I see that face every time I look in the mirror.

I look more like him than I do my mother and it fucking kills me.

"Where have you been?" he asks me, eyes scanning my body. Is he trying to find makeup marks on my person?

"Out." Even if I hadn't been with Lexi, I wouldn't give him more than that.

He throws back his head and laughs. I don't think I've ever hated any sound more. Stopping right next to me, he throws his arm over my shoulder. I have to resist the urge to jerk away from him. "I heard you and Kaylee are still together."

Then his information is outdated. Thank God.

"But"—his eyes, the same color as my own, narrow, and it takes a hell of a lot of willpower to stay where I am—"I have a feeling you weren't with your girlfriend tonight."

I tense before I can think of controlling it. How the fuck . . . then again, that's how my father's mind works. He picks up on the shit no one would ever pick up on. I don't know how he does it.

It's made him a brilliant business man.

And it makes him one of the most dangerous adversaries anyone could ever face.

It's futile to lie to him, let alone straight up foolish. Blatant lies never work on him. I learned that early on in life. Lies somehow set off his internal detector. Half lies, for some reason, tend to sometimes work better on him.

"I wasn't." I hold back from tacking on a "sir". It's been years since I last adhered to that stupid rule of his.

My father continues to study me. "Who was she?"

My reply is quick. It has to be if I want him to believe me. "Fuck if I know." I jerk my shoulder in a shrug. "I didn't bother to ask. Didn't need to."

His laugh grates on my already fried nerves.

Slapping me on the back proudly, he says, "Sometimes you aren't such a disappointment after all." He starts walking toward the entrance of the garage. "You know, for a second I thought you were going to say you were with that Berkman girl. Would have been a shame. I don't want to have to destroy her, son. Her father was my real target. She and her mother can rot on their own for all I care."

I swallow my rage, watching him enter the house. It kills me, but I know I have so much of that man in me. I have the capacity to be as much of a monster as he is.

That's why, as I stand here, I'm more resolved than ever.

My father has to die.

Soon.

<u>kaylee</u>

"You're amazing in bed, babe."

I smirk at Stephen's comment. "I know."

"Honestly, I don't understand why Andrew would want to dump a girl like you."

Hearing that name aggravates me. I turn over on the bed and rise up on my knees before Stephen.

He's draped on my bed, one arm tucked behind his head. Black hair mussed. Light brown eyes content.

Shit, he better be content. I rocked his world and I know it.

I look him up and down. Stephen is sexy as hell and incredible in bed.

But he's not Andrew.

No one is.

A man like that doesn't leave me.

Andrew doesn't seem to know that but he will. Soon.

"You promised me that video, Stephen."

He raises his eyebrow. "I did. But first, I have to know what you plan to do with it."

Gorgeous, but sometimes he seems to be kind of slow. "I'm going to use it to make both Andrew and his bitch pay." Yeah, I've forgiven Andrew his indiscretions in the past. Because, come on, we're meant for each other.

Marrying him will make me the envy of every woman everywhere.

Marrying him will make me twice as rich as I am now.

He always cheated with nameless girls. But now he thinks he can leave me for that pathetic little nobody?

I poke Stephen in the chest. "Give it to me."

"I thought you only wanted to hurt Andrew. This will hurt them both."

Rolling my eyes, I sigh. "Duh. I told you, that's what I want."

He doesn't say anything.

"What aren't you telling me?"

"Nothing babe. I'll give it to you as promised."

Okay, maybe he's not so stupid after all.

Stephen sits up and reaches for his phone. "But you have to promise me something in return."

The nerve. "I don't like stipulations. You promised. And I already fucked you, so I don't owe you anything."

His eyes flash before darkening and becoming lifeless.

Shivers break out all over my skin. I start to move back. His hand flies out and latches onto my arm, squeezing hard. "Stephen, you're hurting me!"

He squeezes harder. "I'll give you this video and you'll do with it what you need to do. But no one can find out that you got it from me."

"Let me go!"

Stephen leans closer, his expressing twisting into something scary. "Do you hear me, Kaylee? No one ever finds out."

"Okay! Okay! Let me go, you fucking psycho!"

He does, his face transforming with a friendly smile. "Good. Now go get your laptop so I can transfer this video."

Shaking, I scramble off the bed.

"Oh, and Kaylee? One more thing. Don't ever, ever call me a psycho again, babe. People tend to get hurt when they call me that."

chapter 32

lexi

present

i googled him.

For the first time in the last seven years, I ran a search on Andrew Drevlow.

I should have left the office. After finishing my work for the day early, I should've just gotten up, left this building, and gone straight home. Maybe then I could have talked myself out of it, convinced myself to ignore the temptation.

It's so cold in here. Has to be. I can't stop shaking.

Can't get the articles and their titles out of my mind, either.

"Andrew Logan Drevlow, heir to Drevlow Systems Incorporated, in a coma after a fiery crash."

"Three weeks later, and Ronald Drevlow's son remains on life support—doctors say chances of survival are minimal."

"One of New Jersey's most prominent heirs awakens from

oma."

"Andrew Drevlow—will he ever walk again?"

It was splashed all over the news for months straight and I never knew.

I became that good at isolating myself.

So Andrew Drevlow almost died six years ago. I don't know the details of the crash, didn't bother reading the articles. I only read the headlines. That was more than enough.

I'm having a violent physical reaction to what I read and it's confusing me. I don't care that he almost died.

I. Don't. Care.

My stomach heaves, as if to say, *"The hell you don't."*

That crash, however it happened, had nothing to do with me. And as far as I'm concerned, it was probably karma well-earned.

The thought feels so wrong. I'm disgusted with myself for thinking it.

Which makes no freaking sense. This is Andrew Drevlow! Why should I feel bad?

Sickened, confused, I grab all my things and leave my office. The elevator ride down is its own special type of hell. I keep expecting to see Andrew and my heart races every time the thought crosses my mind.

My new position came with a reserved parking spot at the lowest level of the building. It seemed convenient at first, but now I'm apprehensive. Surely, Andrew's spot is also down here.

How am I going to avoid bumping into him?

You're not going to avoid it, you dumbass. You work for him!

I'm so preoccupied, that at first, I don't hear my name being called.

"Lexi!"

It's Paul.

Fuck, I don't want to see him. He's here because of me. I didn't ask him to follow me to this company, but I didn't do enough to deter him, either.

With no other option but to face him, I turn.

He jogs up to me. "Are you okay?"

I'm not going to bother answering that question. "Paul, I'm sorry, but I really have to go."

"What's going on between you and Mr. Drevlow?"

A million thoughts swirl around in my head—a million different denials. His question catches me so off guard that it paralyzes me.

Why on Earth would he ask me that?

Paul seems to read my shocked facial expression. "You should've seen him when I mentioned your name. It *killed* him, Lexi."

I shake my head. Denial. Denial. Denial.

Paul's brow furrows, his dark blue eyes worried. "Is he the one, Lexi? Is he the reason I could never truly have you?"

He knows about Stephen. What he did to me. It's the reason he's on this quest for vengeance with me.

But I never, ever told him about Andrew.

"I—I can't talk about this right now. I have to go." Like the coward I am, I run away from him, heading straight to my car.

I'm a mess. Out of control. I was supposed to feel nothing when I saw Andrew again. Instead, I'm feeling too many different things.

It's almost like I'm two steps away from a mental breakdown.

That demon that once possessed me, made me believe I couldn't take my next breath if I didn't have him, is on my heels. It chases me. Torments me.

Reminds me that the addiction never truly went away. It's insidious. A virulent presence deep in my bone marrow.

I'm helpless. Once again drowning in a sickness that has destroyed me one too many times.

It's my fault that I remained on the path leading to Stephen. That I let him convince me he truly hadn't known about the video. Every decision I made at the age of eighteen and onward led me to the pain I endured under Stephen.

Yet, I can't deny that Andrew's actions set me on that path in the first place. His father tricked my father, and then Andrew tricked me. I despise myself for the way I feel, for the fact that I feel anything other than hatred for him.

My brain disengages from my body. Disassociation. I can't deal with all of this. Taking out my keys, I hit the button and unlock my car.

Footsteps reach my ears.

Years of trauma and hypervigilance take over, tensing all my muscles, preparing me for a fight.

"Lexi."

Andrew.

I debate opening the door, jumping into my car, and speeding like a devil out of here.

But I'll have to face him tomorrow, won't I?

Limbs numb, I turn. Concern flares, and it shouldn't. What does it matter that he seems different, that the look in his eyes is abnormal?

Warped, frightening. So intense that heat explodes through my veins, turning a freezing body molten in a second.

He backs me into my car. I shouldn't let him.

I do.

Can't stop it.

I still want this man.

And he knows it.

"You shouldn't look at me like that, Lexi. Not if you want me to keep my hands to myself." He flattens his hands on the window by my head.

I don't look away. This darkness in him is too fascinating to ignore.

He ducks his head, lips grazing mine. "Tell me to move away.

Tell me not to kiss you."

I don't.

I see a flash of a smirk, so similar to the cocky one I remember, before his mouth comes down on my own.

chapter 33

andrew

present

"i need to come, Lexi."

The words are selfish. Self-centered. But that doesn't make them any less true.

I'm lying. They aren't self-centered. This has nothing to do with me. It's all about her.

Those lips.

The way she smells.

Her body ignites my soul. For the first time in almost a decade, the feel of a woman's body actually activates a response in me.

I force her mouth open and rub my tongue against hers roughly. She takes it, all of it, soft little mewls echoing in the back of her mouth.

Yes. Fuck, *yes.*

My hips shove into her, pressing her into the car. Things fall to the floor. What? I don't know and I sure as hell don't care. I yank on the bottom of Lexi's tight black dress. She claws at my blazer, trying to rip it off.

Not close enough. Not close enough.

I grind into her harder, but there's no room between us. Her leg wraps around my hips, trying to bring me in closer.

Shit. I need more.

Grunting, I lift her up, her back sliding along her black Escalade. Both her legs wrap around me, and we're nothing more than a straining, needy mess, our teeth and tongues dueling for dominance.

My cock's wet for her, and I know her pussy's even wetter for me.

Goddamn it, I need to get at it. Need to touch it. Taste it. It's been too long.

"Drew." Lexi struggles in my arms, hips thrusting, clearly searching out her own orgasm. "Drew."

I drop her back on her feet. Her surprised gasp echoes around us. "Where are your fucking keys, Lexi?"

Her gorgeous eyes widen with realization. Shaking, disoriented, she looks around the ground and spots her purse.

"Hurry, Lexi." There's no hiding the wild impatience in my voice. I grab my cock and squeeze it, trying to lessen this insane urge I have to flip her around, push her against the car, and just fuck her until she takes every drop of my come.

Lexi's trembling too hard to properly search through her bag. She looks up at me, eyes falling to where I'm jerking my dick, and her entire world seems to stop.

I moan low under my breath at her hungry stare. I want to step up to her, grab that pony tail, and force her face into my crotch. My dick aches for those lips, her tongue. *"Lexi."*

"I-I . . ." She pulls her eyes away from my dick and looks around frantically.

TWISTED HEARTBREAK

"There," I groan, pointing to where the keys fell next to the tire. By sheer force of will, I let my cock go. It takes even more willpower to wait for her to pick up those keys and hit the unlock button.

As soon as I hear the locks disengage, I pull open the door and rush her inside.

Fuck her purse. Her briefcase. Whatever is inside, either. I'll replace everything if I have to, but I can't wait any longer. She scrambles along the back seat and I follow her inside. I can imagine what I look like as I close the door and crawl over her.

Seven years of obsessively yearning for her have changed me. I've gone fucking crazy over her and the worst part is that I'm aware of it. I know how sick this love has made me. What it's turned me into.

I have no doubt that I look like a monster to her right now. A starving, merciless being that has only one thing on its mind.

"I can't help myself, baby. I'm going to fuck you. Right here. And it's going to be hard. I'm going to hurt you," I warn her, reaching for her smooth, beautiful leg.

She lunges for me before I can, pushing me back against the closed door. My head hits the roof, but she doesn't give a fuck about that. Her fingers pull at my belt, tear at my zipper, reach inside to grab the most painful part of me.

I slam back into the door, practically convulsing. Her hand on my cock feels better than any other woman's pussy. Grinding my teeth, I close my eyes, trying to hold on. Can't explode yet. I want to. Her touch combined with her presence is fucking with my twisted mind in just the right way, messing with my bodily responses.

She mumbles, low, surprised words, invoking a God that can't save her now. I feel her pull me out of my pants, her soft hand caressing me reverently.

And I start to come. Just like that. One ghost caress from Lexi is all it takes for my body to bow backwards against the door as blinding pleasure consumes me.

I'm screaming again. Roaring. Stuck in a vortex of memories and agony.

I've fucked a thousand pussies since I lost her, searching for a single shred of sensation like the kind she can cause in me.

And I found nothing. Nothing but emotional black holes. A world of shame. Hurricanes of anger and madness that grew with every failed fuck. Because none of them were her. None of them could ever compare.

chapter 34

andrew

present

i'm still shuddering against the door and can't bring myself to look down at my girl. My dick's harder than ever, straining in her grasp, and even though I just came, I can feel another one building in my balls.

"I've always wanted to . . ."

Her voice. God, fuck, *help me*.

Behind my closed eyelids, my eyes roll into the back of my head.

She always wanted to what?

Soft, plump, familiar flesh touches the tip of my dick, then parts, sucking me into wet heaven.

My eyes fly open.

"Lexi. Fuck. *Fuck*. What—"

Oh God. Oh God. My girl's head is tilted to the side, her succulent lips open and wrapped around my cock. She's shy, hesitant, but her tongue feels so fucking perfect as she slowly tongues me and takes me in deeper.

A loud inhuman growl is ripped out of me and I arch back into the door. One hand claws at the roof of the car. The other flies down to wrap around her ponytail and hold her to me. Need blinds me and I forget all about her comfort.

Tightening my hand, I force her mouth down on me, sliding all the way into the back of her throat.

She gags around me, a small, shocked sound leaving her.

The feel of her throat constricting around my tip sends me flying over yet another edge.

Painful.

Perfect.

She won't stop gagging around me and each constriction sucks even more come out of me. Tears stream down her face, and I can hear her struggling to breathe above my loud moans.

I can't stop.

Won't stop.

I hold her head to me, her lips wrapped around the base of my dick, and force her to swallow every drop. One last shudder goes through me and I fall limp, my entire body going numb from the back-to-back orgasms.

Lexi pulls back, heaving, gasping.

Worry sparks.

What the fuck did I just do? How could I do that to her? I'm even more of a fucking asshole than I realized.

She wipes at her tear-stained cheeks and licks my come off her lips. "Holy fuck . . . that was so good."

I lunge. Lifting her off the seat, I move her all the way to the other side and force her to lay on her back. She lets me part her legs, watching me with clouded eyes. "You liked that baby? You liked me forcing my cock deep into your throat and filling it with my come?"

She swallows hard and nods.

Oh yeah. This girl is dying to be fucked by me. God damn, that drives me crazy. I reach between her legs and fist her panties.

Her eyes widen and she gasps nervously. There's something different in her eyes now. Something that should worry me.

I'm too far gone to focus on it.

One tug is all it takes for her panties to give way. Her lush, pink pussy grabs all my attention. I barely hear her whimper above the sound of my roaring heart. Her entire body tenses.

Another red flag.

Damn me, I should pay attention. I should listen to the loud warning signals blaring all around me.

But I can't.

My world narrows to the sight of that pussy. I lunge down between her legs, pushing her roughly up against the door to make more room for my body.

Then it's just my lips and her cunt. No soft kisses. No easing her into it. I open my mouth against her and lick her from ass to clit. Lexi jerks, her body silently seizing.

I lick her again, and again, my tongue dipping into her entrance each time.

And it isn't lost on me. There's no barrier.

Someone's been here before me.

Of course they were.

I've forgotten all about my previous suspicions, her fear when I got close to her in her office.

I pull back and my lip curls as a growl leaves me. Grabbing her thighs, I jerk them open wider. It's been seven years. I have no right to expect her to still be a virgin. It makes sense that she didn't wait for me.

I. Don't. Fucking. Care.

"This is mine, you hear me?" I look up at her wide, slightly frightened eyes. Fear. There's no ignoring it now. She's afraid of me. And I don't give a damn about that, either. She *should* be afraid. "I don't give a fuck who had you after I tasted you. Who got to take you. They don't fucking matter because this is mine and it's always belonged to me. But you forgot that, didn't you, Lexi?"

Her lips part and her voice breaks when she tries to say my name. "A-Andrew."

"Yeah. You fucking forgot. But after I'm done with you, you'll never forget again."

chapter 35

andrew
present

i use my thumbs to spread her plump pussy lips open. She's glistening from both her juices and my saliva—the most beautiful cunt I've ever seen.

The tip of my tongue teases her entrance and I almost lose my fucking mind as her core clenches, trying to suck me in. "You need me in this pussy so bad, don't you?" I kiss her pussy softly.

Lexi's eyes roll into the back of her head and her hips churn for more. "Yes. Oh. My. *God*. It's so good, Andrew. Eat my pussy." There's awe in her voice.

None of the men she's ever been with have been able to play this pussy the way I am right now. It's obvious.

God damn it, I'm not going to be able to let her leave this car without slamming my cock in her.

Breaths harsh, I pull back in an effort to regain some form of normalcy. "Baby. We need to get the fuck out of here. I need to get you somewhere with a bed."

"Don't care." She yanks my head back between her legs and slides her slick cunt along my mouth.

I suck her clit in and make out with it, giving her soft, leisurely licks. Her head falls back against the door and her hips move faster.

Every fucking moan seals her fate that much more. She needs me; what I feel goes beyond need.

God forgive me, but I'm going to tear this woman's entire world apart, leaving room for nothing but me.

My fingers tighten around her thighs and I know I'm grabbing her too hard. Every molecule vibrates with this mad hunger, and I bite down on her pussy lip, out of control.

Lexi yelps, back bowing.

She loves that. Loves the pain I can give her.

I never knew I wanted to hurt her, but right now I do. I want us both to ache and bleed for each other as I make her come.

Another bite on her other lip and then I lave her clit with my tongue, up and down, side to side, teasing it until it swells to a painful point.

I devour her pussy at my own pace, ignoring her pleas, the way she moves her hips to get the friction she needs to come.

Possession clamors inside me, choking me. I love her more than I've ever loved her before; I *hate* her for turning me into this.

I suck on her clit hard, punishing her for being so fucking delicious.

Lexi's head rises and her eyes lock with mine—frantic, afraid.

No, *terrified*.

She's so close to coming and she's panicking at the sensation, even as her body tenses, her hips lock up—

"Andrew, no. Please. Wait."

I lick her clit in circles.

Her back arches, her lips parting with a scream.

My name. She's screaming my name over and over, coming violently all over my face.

I slide two of my fingers into her, stuffing her small pussy full. She's creaming, so wet that my fingers are instantly drenched.

I scissor them, spreading her hole open, and press my thumb roughly into her clit.

Her hand slaps the fogged window above her head. Her eyes are squeezed shut, tears leaking down her face and leaving makeup marks on her cheeks.

She's trying to shut me out. Block the intensity of what's happening between us.

I've never been able to block this out, even through all those years of not having her, so she's fucking mistaken if she thinks I'm letting her.

I rear back away from her onto my knees although the height of the car makes it almost impossible.

Her eyes fly open at the loss of my fingers. The devastated need I see in them pacifies me.

I fist my cock and cup my tight balls. "You're getting this. Now."

Shaking, she slides up into a sitting position, eyeing my dick.

And I see it. A perfect reflection of my insanity. A dark, hungry, twisted desire that isn't anywhere near normal.

It gives me pause.

I want her crazy for me. I *need* her like that.

But my girl isn't just crazy for me; she's crazy, *period*. I would know.

There's something really wrong with her.

I let go of my dick and balls.

Lexi reaches forward, fisting my balls and yanking them hard.

My thoughts scramble. I grab her wrist to stop her. Have to concentrate. She's more important.

Lexi fists my dick with her other hand and tugs it roughly. Like she hates me and loves me as much I do her, and she needs to make me feel the bite of that all over my body.

Too late. It's in my soul.

"Baby, wait, we need—"

Outside the car, a loud, blaring sound goes off.

She falls back, gasping, terror in her eyes. "My phone."

Her what?

Half-turning, she opens the door behind her and practically pours backwards out of the car. The way she runs around to the other side, where her purse still is, tells me everything I need to know.

That unholy ring tone is coming from her phone.

And whatever it is, it means that something really bad is happening.

chapter 36

andrew
present

i exit the car and bend down quickly to stick the small tracker to the bottom of her car.

Yes, I'm breaking the law.

Yes, I plan on stalking her.

No, I don't give a fuck how wrong that is.

That ring tone was set to be loud and obnoxious for a reason.

It's a warning. Something's going on.

Lexi's speaking in a hurried, hushed tone I can't fully make out. I think I hear *medicine, testing, possibilities*.

I hurry around the side of the car, determined to figure out what the hell this is about.

"I'm on my way," Lexi says just as I get close enough and she ends the call. She tries to rush past me to pick up her purse.

I block her path.

Frantic, she tries *pushing* me out of her way.

Silly girl. I finally have her back in my life. Nothing's moving me.

I grab her arms. "Look at me."

Wide, blown pupils focus on my face.

"What's going on?"

She rips her arms out of my grasp. "None of your business."

"I waited seven fucking years to find you. You just choked on my dick and swallowed every drop of my come. Everything about you is my business. Understand?"

She gives me the mother of all nasty glares and storms around me. As she bends down to shove everything back in her purse, I move to block the driver's side so she can't get in.

I'm pushing too hard. Too fast. She's like a scared little kitten I have to coax to my side, but the panic in her expression has hijacked my common sense.

"I'll fix everything," I tell her. "Tell me what's wrong and I swear to God I'll raze the whole world down and rebuild it for you in order to fix all your problems."

Purse in her arms, she stumbles back away from me, her eyes wide and disbelieving. She tries to hide it but I see it.

Despair.

Longing.

Hope.

I know the look of someone who considers themselves utterly alone in the world and that's it. She shutters her expression and ducks her head.

Too late. My heart's broken wider for her than ever. I'm bleeding at her fucking feet and I know she can't even see it. "Tell me." I step closer and reach out my hand. "I'll fix it. Right the fuck now."

"You can't."

That tone of hers perfectly mimics what I saw in her eyes before.

She might not know it, but she's broadcasting her need loud and clear.

She won't let me in.

She doesn't trust me.

I know she has every right not to.

But it isn't just me. Lexi has become an island unto herself. Loneliness radiates off her as strong as her need for help. This woman doesn't trust anyone anymore. She doesn't let anyone in.

And I know, with absolute certainty, that Menahan is as much to blame as I am. "What did he do to you, Lexi?"

She scoffs and tries to bodily move me out of her way. "I don't have time for this shit." That guarded anger is back.

By asking her that question, I gave her a reason to completely close herself off again.

Fine. She doesn't have to tell me. Eventually, I will find out.

I move out of her way. "I'm here. Whatever you need. My entire fortune is at your disposal."

Another scoff and her door slams closed. Two seconds later, she's peeling out of the parking lot at a speed that worries me.

I run to my Pagani Huayra and jump in. In the blink of an eye, I have my phone clipped to the dashboard and the tracking app fired up. I connect the coordinates to my onboard GPS and slam my foot down on the gas.

It takes me less than thirty seconds to catch up to her thanks to the monster engine in this car. I slow down once I have her in my sights, knowing that this car is way too fucking flashy not to catch attention.

If she so much as catches a glimpse of this car, she'll know she's being tailed.

If she remembers anything about me and my obsession for ridiculously expensive, high-tech vehicles, she'll know it's me.

I ease up on the gas again, letting her gain more distance. I won't lose her thanks to the tracker so I can afford to risk it.

It isn't until she blows a *third* red light—and I'm forced to do the same—that I mentally hit Defcon Five.

This shit, whatever it is, is worse than I imagined.

And I realize that Lexi is gunning it for the highway leading out of Jersey City.

Luck must be watching out for us both. At the speed we're driving, it's a miracle we aren't pulled over.

Lexi swerves in and out of cars in her haste. I don't do so, but only because I can see which direction she's heading and I don't want to call any more attention to myself by doing the same.

When she flies toward the exit to Newark, my heart drops into my stomach. I don't know if it's this insane, almost cosmic connection I have with the girl, but suddenly I have a really big feeling about where she's heading.

The towering, huge buildings that make up the Hackensack University Medical Center come into view, and I know without a doubt that that's where Lexi's going.

chapter 37

andrew
present

i'm parked in one of the parking lots with my cell phone up to my ear and my eyes glued on the main building of the hospital.

Lexi ran in there about five minutes ago. There hasn't been a chance for me to install a tracker on her phone, and for some reason I . . . I don't want to.

I have the one on her car and that's bad enough. I'm already invading her privacy to a heinous extent.

It's not just the tracker. It's my current line of questioning. "Who's in there Uncle Richard?" I ask again.

"What makes you think I know the answer to that question, Drew?"

"Don't fucking lie to me. We're the biggest donors to this hospital. We practically own the fucking place. Now, tell me who the fuck is in there."

Silence. The kind of silence that screams guilt louder than any admission ever could. "I can't, Drew. Something's very wrong with you when it comes to that woman."

I don't bother disagreeing with his assessment because it's dead-on. "Send me a copy of the contract then." I have a feeling the information I'm after will be on there.

"No."

"Why?"

"Same reason."

So the information *is* on there. "You do know I'm your fucking boss now, right?"

A few more minutes of silence. This time, instead of guilt, I feel his disbelief leaking through the connection.

"What did you just say to me?"

Ah, the deadly side of Richard Drevlow.

He's a decent human being, for the most part. But that's only half of who he is. In the end, there's an evil darkness encoded in our DNA. A stain that passes down from generation to generation.

Uncle Richard and I, we try to be kind. To be different than our coding tells us to be.

But at the end of the day, a wolf is still a wolf.

A lion is still a lion.

And the devil is still the devil.

We can play pretend all we want, we're all still monsters.

And I'm a bigger one than my uncle can ever be. Losing Lexi did that to me.

"You heard me. You put me in this position. You wanted me here. Well, now here I am, and as your boss, I demand that you send me that contract directly to my inbox."

"She really is the reason you went crazy."

"That and our genetics, I suppose."

He barks out a surprised laugh and my lips twitch in response.

His voice when he speaks, however, has no trace of humor in it. "You can't go back down that path."

"I won't."

"A junkie is always mentally a junkie. You know that."

"I was chasing her." It's true. Every time I slid that needle into a vein, I was chasing the feeling of having her. Ridiculous, I know that now. No drug could ever compare.

"Andrew, you are the head of this company now. You can't go back to that lifestyle."

"She's back in my life. I'm sure this contract is iron-clad and long enough to keep her here as long as I need her"—long enough to get her to forgive me and love me again— "so trust me. I won't be touching that shit again."

"Give me five minutes then."

Good. He knows his place.

I'd like to say it bothers me to have to subjugate him like this, but nothing gets in the way of me helping Lexi.

Besides, I have too much Drevlow blood in me to care about such things.

I hang up the phone and stare at the entrance to the hospital. I have a bad feeling about what's—who's—in that hospital. For Lexi to run here like this, it has to be someone beyond important.

I remember Mrs. Berkman. What she looked like—an exact but older replica of Lexi. Her heart—as loving and kind as her daughter's.

She was so nice to me when I was a boy.

No. It can't be her. I refuse to believe it. Life can't be so cruel as to deal that blow to my Lexi.

But yes it can. I know that. I learned that once and for all the day I lost her.

The memory comes over me suddenly, taking me back to one of the most fucked up days of my life.

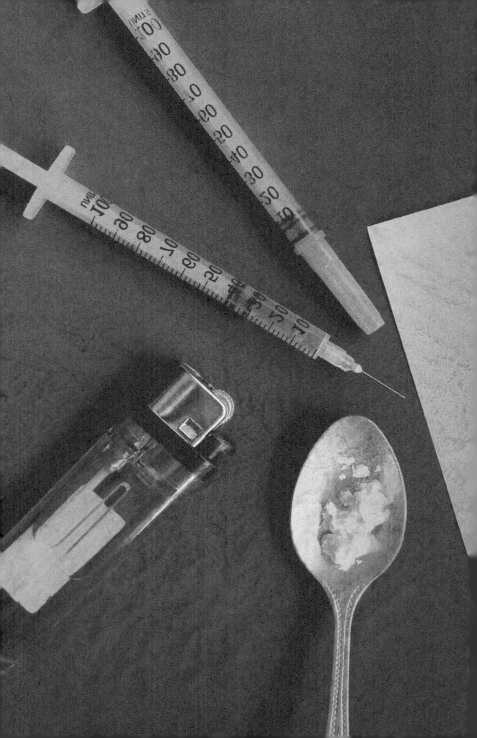

chapter 38

andrew
7 years ago

i t's the perfect fucking morning.

Yeah, I know, make fun of me. Laugh all you want. But I swear to God I heard birds singing outside my window and shit when I woke up.

The first thing I did when I opened my eyes? Smile like a motherfucking lovesick fool.

The second? Hit up my girl, wish her a good morning, and told her how much I fucking miss her.

Kaylee's been blowing up my phone since last night.

I don't care. She doesn't stop that shit and I'll end up blocking her. The days of life getting between Lexi and I are way over.

I'm literally whistling as I get ready for school. Rushing through my morning routine, I do the bare minimum when it comes to grooming and get ready to bolt out the door.

A knock on my door makes me pause.

"It's me, honey."

Mom.

I smile at her and grab my backpack. On my way out the door, I pause to give her a kiss on the cheek.

She grabs my arm. "Your father is demanding to see you." The barely hidden disdain in her voice is sad, man. Really sad. I don't know jack shit about marriage, but I know that theirs is just all kinds of fucked up. "Mom, I love you, but I'm not in the mood to see him right now."

I'm high off Lexi. That's all I care to feel today.

"Honey, he isn't giving you or me a choice in the matter." Her brown eyes search mine. "Did you do something or is this him being his typical self?"

"I didn't—" Unless Kaylee, that whining little girl, called him and told him I left her.

Fuck.

Whatever. I was going to have to deal with this eventually.

I kiss my mom on the cheek and head down the hall without saying another word. It takes me five minutes to make it downstairs to his office.

The door's closed. Of course it is. He wants everyone to knock, and then wait for him to deem us worthy of entry.

Damn. I just want to get into my car and head to school. To Lexi.

I knock on the door, grinding my teeth together. He doesn't answer. I grind my teeth harder and wait a full minute before knocking again.

This vanity-filled motherfucker is going to make me late.

"Come in!" Short. Clipped. Displeasure? Evident.

I take a deep breath, pray for the self-control not to end him, and open the door.

The lord and master is sitting behind his huge, ridiculous desk, fingers steepled. The utter disgust in his eyes does nothing to me. I've been seeing it for too long to be fazed by it.

"Good morning," I say like a polite little robot, keeping my expression neutral.

"Shut the fuck up and close the door."

Oh, he's so educated when he wants to be.

More like a piece of shit right off the streets.

I close the door and wait right where I am, knowing that he'll tell me when he wants me to come close.

"You want me to destroy that little Ms. Berkman, don't you?"

A primal, dangerous reaction explodes in my cells, and I have to lock every muscle to control it.

No one threatens Lexi. No one hurts her. *No one.* One day, this asshole is going to learn that the hard way.

For a few moments, I'm worried he found out about me and her, and my mind races to come up with believable lies.

But no, he didn't. His gaze is too questioning. This piece of crap is fishing for a reaction.

Kaylee called him. I know she did.

"This has nothing to do with that little Ms. Nobody," I say, surprised at how convincing I sound. Then again, when one has to play a role their whole life, eventually it comes by rote.

"Oh? This week she's little Ms. Nobody?"

"She's fucking some lowlife in the Chess club." Fuck, man. That lie *burns* in the back of my throat.

My father throws his head back and laughs. "Ah. So the slut finally reveals herself."

Let it go. What he says means nothing. Fuck his opinion. It doesn't matter what he says about her 'cause it'll never be true.

"There's nothing worse than a whore that can't control herself."

Fucking double standard of his. Hell, his entire identity is a double standard. "That's very true, father. Which is why I'm sure you'll understand why I broke up with Kaylee." My father's head snaps down and his eyes narrow. "What? Did you think I wouldn't know she rushed to call you?"

"What are you saying, boy?"

"I will never marry a slut that can't stop guzzling other men's come left and right."

chapter 39

andrew

7 years ago

my father's head tilts back with shock. His eyes narrow suspiciously and I can already tell he doesn't believe me before he even speaks. "Kaylee wouldn't behave like that."

"Of course she would. She isn't my mother." It's a deliberate jab. A reminder that he doesn't deserve a good woman like my mother. A woman that remains faithful to him only because he's her husband, not because he deserves it.

"Kaylee was raised to be better. And watch your words with me, boy."

I shrug. "She was raised to be better but she isn't. If you don't believe me, go ahead. Spy on her." I know he has the means to do so, too. "But I deserve better than her. A woman is supposed to do right by her husband at all times. She can't even be faithful to me while I'm her boyfriend."

Throwing my father's words back in his face is a strategic move. I don't believe I deserve better, but my father will. Whatever he believes about me personally, his philosophy is still the same: a man can do whatever he wants. A woman must behave and be good to that man regardless.

Chauvinistic, misogynistic, antiquated bullshit. I know. But if I can use it to play him, I will.

It fucking scares me how much I'm like him sometimes.

"I'm going to look into this." There's a silent fury in my father's eyes. I've just ruined Kaylee's life by doing this.

Better her than Lexi. Sorry.

"You do that." I spin around and walk out of his office.

"Don't think this gives you an excuse to go after that Berkman girl!" he calls after me.

"Jesus Christ, no one even said her name!" I yell back and keep it moving. My blood pounds hot through my veins.

What I wouldn't give to once, just once, slam my fist into that man's mouth.

I rush into my convertible and speed out of the driveway. Twenty minutes 'til school starts. Damn it, I'm cutting it close, and I really, really want to spend time with Lexi before I go inside.

Although I'm driving like a criminal, and I know it's dangerous, I pull out my cell and dial her number.

My girl answers on the first ring. "Drew?"

"Of course, baby. Who else would it be?" The fact that she picked up so quickly when she saw my number has me high as hell on happiness.

She giggles and I swear my fucking toes curl. "I can barely hear you. Is that the wind I hear?"

I'm driving over a hundred, all windows down. Of course the sound of all that air is messing with the reception. I slow down just enough to free my other hand for a few seconds and raise all the windows.

Once they're up, I push down on the gas and break a hundred again. "Better?"

"Drew, stop speeding. I'm worried about you."

And I love you like crazy, girl. The response is stuck in my throat, where it belongs. Now's not the time. Not yet. *But soon,* I promise myself. "I can't help it that I'm dying to see you."

Another adorable giggle. "But if you get hurt, we won't be able to see each other at all."

"Just wait for me where we always meet up. I should be there in less than ten."

She agrees and hangs up the phone.

I hang up as well, completely oblivious to everything but my need to reach her.

The sound of a cop siren makes me jump in my seat.

Fuck. Fuck. Fuck!

Pulling over is the last thing I want to do, but what choice do I have? If I try to lose him, I'll end up in a cop chase and no doubt in jail right after.

Frustrated, I flip the turn signal, and pull over to the side of the road. The cop approaches the car and gives me the usual *"Do you know how fast you were going?"* spiel.

I play my part of repentant young man and give him all my identification. I let him give me the speeding ticket without saying a word to the contrary.

Fuck paying it. I have more than enough money not to care about that. But I need him to finish giving me the damn thing, stat.

Thanks to him, I make it to school almost fifteen minutes late. My entire grade has already been pulled into the auditorium for one of the year-end announcements.

I'll have to find Lexi later.

Walking into the dark auditorium, I freeze dead in my tracks, sounds I remember so fucking well blasting out of all of the speakers. *"Andrew! Oh . . . you're . . . I'm coming . . . uh!"* Eyes wide, I stare at the front of the stage, at the video projecting. Me. Lexi. Us. What happened last night. *Our private moment.* I stagger back, rage burning my mind.

The lights blaze on and all hell breaks loose.

chapter 40

andrew

present

four pages. That's how far into the complicated contract I have to read before I find what I need.

Under the Mutuality of Obligations section. Fifth one down. There, I see the beginning of a multi-page agreement of one of the obligations my company is under in return for Lexi's employment with us.

Medical care.

Extensive.

Expensive.

Ongoing until either we find a cure for the patient . . .

Or the patient dies.

I see the name of the patient we're paying to treat, and I have to close my eyes to contain the painful shock that goes through me.

No. Shit, no. She's all my girl has left. She already suffered so much after what my father did to her.

Once, a long time ago, she was like a second mother to me. Back when I was young and was allowed to go spend time in the Berkman's house.

I shake my head and go back to reading the contract, searching for some sign of what she's being treated for.

But, of course, there's none. The contract itself wouldn't detail that. The only way to find out is to get into the medical records.

Or speak to the patient herself.

I can't go in there while Lexi is still visiting. I'll have to wait until she leaves.

So option one it is.

Bringing my phone to my ear, I call one of my faithful employees in Lexi's department. Finn went to school with me and Lexi, and he was by my side all these years. He saw it all. The rise. The fall. My long, dark flirtation with death. He knows everything.

And he's proven time and time again he's one of the only people I can trust. "Do you know how hard it was to hide myself from Lexi? I'm gone three days and come back to find her working here!" No hello. No, hey how are ya? As usual, Finn just jumps straight to business. Business being him haranguing me, of course.

"Why were you hiding from her?" I ask, praying for patience. I don't have time for this. The information I need is of the utmost importance. But if I don't humor him, I won't be getting anything out of him.

"What do you mean why? Did you tell me I could waltz on up to her and reintroduce myself after all these years?"

"I didn't know you needed my permission."

"Hello? Contractual obligation. And best friend obligation as well. I'm supposed to check in with you in regards to every step of this obsessive, sick, twisted plan of yours."

I sigh and rub the space between my eyebrows. Like I said, he's beyond loyal.

He's also annoying as all hell.

"Finn, you have permission to introduce yourself to Lexi. Finn, you also don't have permission to tell her anything of what I'm up to."

"Oh, you mean the stalking her part?"

I roll my eyes up to the heavens. "Yes, and anything pertaining to that. On that note, I need you to hack into the Hackensack Medical server."

The sound of his fingers flying over the keyboard reaches me through the phone. "What am I looking for?"

"Eliana Berkman. I need to know what she's in there for and what her treatment entails."

"Done." Just like that, my phone vibrates, and I know it's my inbox alerting me to the receipt of the file.

"Remind me not to make you my enemy," I say.

"Remind yourself."

Chuckling, I hang up the phone and download the massive files. Mrs. Berkman's diagnoses is right at the beginning of her medical record.

AIDS.

Confused, I read on. The woman I remember wasn't the type to sleep around. Unless she met someone who had it and didn't know before sleeping with them?

One line catches my attention. **New Strain Unidentified in CDC Databases.** A sick feeling of dread twists my stomach. No. He's a sick bastard, but he can't be this fucked up.

Of course he can.

I fire off a text to Finn.

Drew: Find a way inside Menahan's medical department. Mainly their pharmaceuticals. I want to know what he's experimenting on in there.

It's nothing more than a novelty confirmation. I already know for a fact that he's capable of doing this.

And what better way to control my girl? Eliana is everything to Lexi. *Everything.*

For the last nine hours, I've been going crazy wondering why she would end up working for Stephen.

Now I know.

Just as I know who's the head of his medicinal and pharmaceutical branch.

Fucking Barnard.

He could have spared himself what I have planned for Kaylee and Stephen. Despite his involvement in what went down all those years ago, I might have turned the other cheek.

If what I suspect is true . . . if they did to Eliana what I think they did . . .

What am I saying? I know they did.

I send one last text to Finn and sit back to wait for Lexi to exit the hospital.

Drew: Start files on Barnard Wellington and Kaylee Whittacker. I want everything. Leave nothing out.

chapter 41

andrew

7 years ago

i can't fucking see past the rage pumping through my veins. Teachers rush to turn off the video. Students are talking among themselves so loud that the sound is almost a roar in the air.

I can't spot Lexi anywhere. Can't see any of her friends.

Need to find her. She has to be so embarrassed. So hurt.

Who fucking did this?

Even as I ask myself that question, the answer is painfully obvious.

And then, I see him. Sneaking out the exit on the other side of the auditorium. Laughing and high-fiving Barnard.

Stephen.

They did this.

I slam back out the way I came and head out of the school. That exit leads to the fields on the other side of the building.

Single-minded in my rage, I ignore everyone that turns to stare at me.

One guy comes up to me, laughing and holding up his hand to high-five me. "Dude! You nailed the untouchable one *and* got it on tape!"

Is that what everyone believes? That *I* did this?

Growling, I slam my fist into the guy's face. He crumbles like a house of cards.

I don't know him. Don't give a fuck about him.

People around me stop talking. A few even gasp. I step over the guy and continue on my way around the school.

I turn right, walking down the path next to the football field, and see those two pieces of shit no more than ten feet from the auditorium exit.

I take off running straight at Stephen. More people dash out of my way. One of them even screams, "Stephen! Bro, he's coming right at you!"

It's too late.

Stephen turns, eyes wide—

I tackle him to the ground and slam my fist into his face.

One hit isn't enough.

It'll never be.

He'll die for doing this to my girl.

I wail on him, one hit after the other.

Someone comes up behind me and tries to yank my arms back. I know who it is without seeing. Jerking my arms out of his grip, I slam my elbow back.

I hit Barnard's midsection. A burst of air leaves him.

Stephen, his nose and lips bleeding, reaches up to wrap his hands around my neck. He tries to buck me off.

Ignoring the fact that he's choking me, I growl like an animal and start raining blows on his face again.

"Drew! Drew, please, stop!" It's Kaylee. She's pulling at me, getting between us somehow. I don't give a damn about her, but at the same time, I don't want to hurt her.

She breaks Stephen's hold on me and pulls at my shoulders until I rise. I shrug out of her grip and slam my foot into Stephen's chest when he tries to get up.

"Kaylee, stay the fuck out of this. I don't want to hurt you."

Stephen laughs, his teeth coated with blood. Spitting on the floor, he sneers up at me. "She's the one that played the video in front of everyone."

"He's lying!"

I turn my head slowly, eyes narrowing in her direction. The tremor in her voice. The fear in her eyes. "You fucking bitch," I hiss.

"Fuck you!"

Fisting my hands is the only way I can keep myself from grabbing that disgusting, envious bitch. The only way to stop myself from hurting her. "You listen to me well, you good for nothing low life."

Several people inhale sharply around us.

I turn fully to face Kaylee and start advancing on her. "It won't be now. It won't be tomorrow. I'll leave you wondering when. But trust me, one day, *I'm going to fucking ruin you.*"

Her face goes pale at my threat.

I hear Stephen get to his feet and turn just in time to catch the punch he's aimed at my head. I land a left uppercut straight into his stomach. He stumbles away from me and throws up.

All of a sudden, I'm grabbed roughly from behind and it's obvious it isn't Kaylee this time. Too much strength. Too much mass.

I struggle to break free as another school security guard forces Stephen to stand up straight.

They start dragging us back toward the school. I struggle even harder because now I'm not just thinking of killing Stephen.

I need to find Lexi. I try to force the security guard holding me to let me go.

He pushes me toward the front of the school. Police cars are parked outside, their lights flashing.

If I try to escape, it's going to be worse for me. They'll keep me from Lexi longer. We pass Finn, who's eyes me with a worried expression in his gray eyes.

"Find her!" I scream to him as I'm being led toward the officers. "Make sure she's alright!" The only comfort I have is that he'll know who I'm talking about. Now, I can only pray he can get to her before I'm released.

chapter 42

andrew

present

Lexi didn't leave for over two hours. Now, I'm the one at the front desk, asking for a pass to go see Eliana Berkman.

It takes the lady in front of me no more than a few seconds to pull up the name—and I'm hoping in those seconds. Fucking *praying*. Life's already been too cruel to my Lexi. I'll give anything for it to not be her mother up there.

I know what the damned contract said, but come on man, please, if you're up there, let it not be Mrs. Berkman . . .

The older, blonde woman grabs a pass and hands it to me, saying, "Room 503. That's the—"

"The intensive care unit. I know." My entire chest feels heavy with disappointment. Yet, fuck. I know what I read in that contract. Was I really stupid enough to hope it wasn't true?

Yeah. Yeah, I was.

"Been here often?" The lady asks me nicely.

I nod, taking the pass. She has no idea who I am. What I do for this hospital.

Running a hand over my head, I walk over to the elevator and wait with everyone else. More people that don't know who I am. More of them that have no idea what's happening inside me.

I want to call Lexi. Fuck me, I want to chase her down and find a way to erase whatever horrors she's been through.

If Menahan did this to her, he's probably done more. Much worse.

Her sad, scared eyes flash through my mind—

No. Not now. I can't think about this. Can't assume.

There's a vicious darkness in the pit of my brain. It's laughing at me. Telling me it's only a matter of time.

If what I think is true, I know what type of monster I'm about to become.

And for her, it'll all be worth it.

I'll kill the whole motherfucking world in her name, if I must.

Inside the elevator, I'm fidgety. Darkness continues to spread, now within my veins, telling me it knows the truth. All I have to do is listen.

I can't. Grinding my teeth, I shove all of it into a corner of my mind.

Compartmentalize. Ignore. Refocus on the present. All tricks of a damaged boy turned into a damaged man.

Tricks of a past-junkie that learned to live with his crippling addictions—well, one of them. The heroin cravings I can deal with and ignore.

The cravings for Lexi have slowly driven me mad.

But I'm not so mad that I've lost my compassion for innocent people. Eliana? She's one of them. And before I head out to find her daughter, I'm going to get to the bottom of what happened to her.

I get off the elevator and head straight for the nurse's desk. When I ask her where the room I'm looking for is, she smiles brightly at me.

"You know Mrs. Berkman?"

I nod, but it isn't enough. She wants details. I see it in her beaming eyes. "Since I was a kid."

Her smile somehow widens. "Her daughter is the only one that comes to visit. It's so nice to see a new face."

She leads me toward the room, and my heart beats harder. Faster. Painful.

I loved that woman once. Almost as much as I love my own mother. For a few years, while my father was still playing buddy-buddy with Mr. Berkman, I was allowed to be close to Lexi.

Allowed to go over to their place.

Eliana took care of me. Welcomed me. Gave me affection. My mother always suffocated me in it, but it was nice to get more of it out there in the world.

When your father is a piece of shit, and the people in your social class seem to mimic his behaviors, you start to believe there isn't much good in the world.

Eliana is that good. She had the inner light that was so brilliant it made me happier just to be in her presence.

An inner light her daughter inherited.

The nurse steps aside so I can walk into the room.

I do, each step becoming slower and slower. My eyes bounce off all the machines. The wires.

The frail, thin, blonde woman lying in the bed.

The oxygen mask over her face.

Gray eyes I know so well, eyes her daughter also inherited, open to focus on me. They widen, then water, and my name leaves her in a frail but happy whisper, *"Drew."*

And I know. I know she believes I'm innocent. That whatever happened, she knows I'm still that kid that fell in love with her daughter and would rather die than do her harm.

My knees buckle beneath me and my upper body falls onto the bed next to her as I start sobbing, torn apart by the sight of her like that.

chapter 43

lexi
present

That big, monstrous cock nearly choked me to death. The taste of him? Vicious. Merciless in its ability to make a woman addicted.

His voice coming . . . It's even deeper now than it was seven years ago.

Or was it something else that made his voice lower to an almost brutal degree? When he screamed for me, his come spurting down my throat, the tone of his voice was a perfect match to the maddened look in his eyes.

"Stop!" I slam my hand on the steering wheel, vision blurred with tears.

My mom's taken yet another turn for the worse. The doctors don't know how long they'll be able to keep her alive. So, *why the fuck am I stuck thinking of Andrew's cock?*

The answer is so simple, disgustingly obvious, and I've never loathed myself more than I do now.

You still want him, Lex.

Fucking stupid bitch that I am.

But . . . I've never felt pleasure with anyone but him. Only three men have touched me in my life. First, him. Then, Stephen raped me.

By the time I got to Paul, I had nothing left to give.

Or so I thought.

Andrew fucking manhandled me in the back of this truck. Ragdolled me. Forced me to take every ounce of pleasure he could force out of my body.

And, instead of locking up or zoning out—instead of recalling every traumatizing instant of all the times Stephen abused me—I became nothing more than an aching, pounding, empty hole.

One that would have given everything in this entire universe to be filled by that juicy, swollen dick, and pumped full of Andrew's come.

I start crying harder. "There's something wrong with you, girl. Something really wrong with you." Wiping at my tears, I struggle to get myself under control.

I *need* to be in control. I'm finally in a better place to help my mom. We might not have much time left, but Drevlow Systems has an even larger pharmaceuticals division than Menahan does.

They can save my mom. I have to believe that. But that means I have to keep my shit straight and deliver some good shit to both Mr. Drevlows to get them to agree to pour more money into helping my mom.

Does Andrew know about her yet? The thought is occurring to me for the first time.

I scoff at my obviously spreading idiocy. Of course he knows. There's no way he hasn't read the contract.

Frantic, I wonder if he'd be amiable to helping my mom out *before* I start handing in any real work. Maybe if I go to him and

TWISTED HEARTBREAK

plead with him, he'll find it in him to help the woman that has always cared for him so much?

Yeah fucking right. This is Ronald Drevlow's son. A man that has already proven what a cold-hearted, vicious manipulator he can be.

No matter what my mother thinks, how much she's continued to defend him throughout the years, I can't forget the truth.

But what the fuck am I going to do then?

Work hard. Work my ass off.

Give Andrew the thing both of us want—Menahan's ruin.

It won't be soon enough. You have to try! I don't know why my retarded brain believes that beseeching Andrew is an option—

Fuck it. It truly is my only option.

Cursing, I take the first exit off the highway and pull off the road as soon as I can. My hands are shaking as I take my phone out of my purse.

His number wasn't given to me.

My heart sinks as that realization sets in.

Dear God, please let him still be at work. Let anyone still be there. It's late, I know, but someone has to pick up the phone. *Please.*

Andrew doesn't have an assistant yet, so when I ask the main reception for him, they transfer me straight through to his main line.

It goes to voicemail.

No. No. I actually need you right now, you untrustworthy bastard.

I hang up and call corporate again. This time, I ask for his uncle, who does have an assistant. She gives me a hard time about transferring me, but as soon as I tell her it has to do with the Providence project, she has no problem doing as I ask.

I grind my teeth to refrain from calling her out on her idiocy.

"Hello, Ms. Berkman?"

"Where's your nephew?" I ask, not wasting any time.

BOOK ONE

The silence on his end gives me pause.

"I . . . I believe he left to run an important errand."

He's *lying* to me. And, considering he's a Drevlow, I'm not surprised. "Give me his cell phone."

"I can't, Ms. Berkman. If you need to speak with him about something *work-related*, you can speak with him in the morning."

"You don't understand—"

"No, Ms. Berkman. You don't understand. We need you at this company, and besides, he won't let me get rid of you now, but I want to make something very clear to you. You almost killed him once; I will not allow you to get close to him and destroy him once again. Do I make myself clear?"

chapter 44

andrew

present

eliana is caressing the back of my head soothingly, her movements weak.

I'm sobbing into this mattress like a fucking idiot. Taking a deep breath, I raise my head and meet her stare.

She tries to speak.

I shake my head and wipe my face clean. "Don't. It's okay."

She shakes her head *no* and a tear slides down her cheek. "No. It's not." Her voice is so fucking frail. As if it's costing her all her energy to just utter those words.

"I know. But I'm going to fix this, you hear me? I won't leave you like this."

Her smile breaks my heart. "I know that, now. Seeing you. Here. But . . ." She pauses and stares up at the ceiling. "For so long, I was convinced that you had turned out like your father."

"In some ways, I'm worse," I confess.

"No, Drew. The monsters? The real ones? They're out there. He's . . . one of them."

"Stephen," I growl that name like the curse it is.

"He ruined her."

The words are so weak, so feeble, that I almost don't hear them. "*What*?" My heart is pounding. A cold sweat spreads. Is she confirming what I suspect? That barely formed, homicidal-instinct inducing thought that I haven't allowed myself to fully entertain?

Eliana opens her mouth. Before she can repeat herself, her breath wheezes and she begins coughing uncontrollably.

It's so bad her frail body seems to be seizing on the bed.

Shit. Shit. Fuck. I jump up and press the button for the nurse. Then, I run to the door and yank it open. "Nurse! Doctor! Someone get over here!"

They do. Three nurses and a man I remember very well run inside and rush to Mrs. Berkman's bedside.

I can do nothing but stand here, hands squeezing my head, as they try to adjust her oxygen.

Her upper body arches off the bed and her next cough gives way to a frightening, wheezing sound.

The heart monitor goes crazy.

"Nurse, get me a chest tube!" The doctor yells.

No. No. No. I know what that means. Fuck. I can't believe this is happening. God, please help her. *Please.*

One nurse runs to the cabinets along the wall, grabs a blue, see-through bag, runs back to the doctor, and rips the bag open.

The doctor snaps medical gloves on. Another of the nurses comes up to him, wheeling a small metal tray. On the tray is a metal bowl that she pours a dark purple liquid into.

Within seconds the third nurse has opened another sterile package containing steel medical tongs.

The entire time Eliana is practically shaking from the force of her coughs and the struggle to breathe.

The doctor raises her hospital gown, exposing her side. Using the medical tongs, he dips a large cotton ball in the purple liquid and sterilizes Eliana's side. He injects her with what I assume is an anesthetic.

Any doubt I was struggling to hold on to about what's happening collapses.

Just like her lung.

Her lung has fucking collapsed and *I'm standing here watching them do a chest tube insertion.*

I'm not weak in the face of blood, or gore even, but this is Lexi's mother.

Lexi's mother whose lung just collapsed and if they don't force a tube into her chest, she's going to die.

Right here.

In front of me.

I'm terrified.

And beyond fucking homicidal.

The doctor uses a scalpel to make a small incision in her side. One of the nurses places the leakage drainage machine at the doctor's feet.

I finally turn away. If I don't, the chaos of my unholy rampage will tear through this entire state. A hurricane of bloody carnage that will lead right to Menahan's door.

My mind checks out. For how long? I don't know. A tap on my shoulder jerks me out of my daze.

When I turn, I see Dr. Aaberg behind me.

Wait. The heart monitor is beeping normally. She was stabilized?

I look behind the doctor and see Eliana on the bed, her breathing regulated.

That fucking thick tube inserted into her side.

Her watery, gray eyes stare at me with kindness. Maybe even affection. Me, the piece of shit that barely deserves it.

"I'm going to save you." The vow is gritty. Like broken glass being shoved through cement. But it's powerful. Honest.

There are very few things I've ever truly committed to in life, but when I have, it's been with every ounce of my fucking soul.

She knows it. Her watery smile, behind that oxygen mask, is full of gratitude.

"Mr. Drevlow, I didn't know you know Mrs. Beckman—"

I interrupt Dr. Aaberg. "In your office. Now. We need to speak."

chapter 45

<u>andrew</u>
present

What's that saying? There's no rest for the wicked? I guess that's true. It's 2:45am and here I sit, in the back of a nondescript black Honda in Leonia, half an hour away from the very center of Manhattan.

A half hour and Finn sitting next to me, fidgety as fuck. "Calm the hell down," I tell him, scanning the quiet streets before me.

"Calm the hell down? We're here meeting a *government agent* that just happens to be deep under cover in the motherfucking *Solntsevskaya Bratva*, and you want me to calm the fuck down?"

I glare at him. "You wanted to come. You *insisted*."

His gray eyes narrow, filled with what seems like hatred. "I'm not letting you get yourself killed!"

"I'm one of the most prominent businessmen in the world—"

"Who's planning on handing over another very prominent

business man to the *fucking Russian mafia*!"

His hysterics are nothing new to me. Still, I wish he'd calm the fuck down before this supposed agent gets here. "Actually, I'm handing him over to an undercover agent—"

"Who plans on handing Barnard over to the Russians to solidify his cover even more—oh, and I'm not stupid either. I *know* you plan to be there when they off him."

"Actually—"

A finger is jammed in my face. "No! Just no! You're not saying it and you're certainly not doing it. You will not participate in his actual death!"

My silence makes him gape.

He hisses out a curse and falls back into his seat, yanking at his dirty blond hair. "Do you realize what you're doing?"

I open my mouth to answer.

He shushes me. "No. I'm serious. You used your government connections and *my* ultra-superior hacking skills to get in contact with this guy. Now you're dipping your big fat toe in the mafia pool and want to dunk it in a bucket of blood as you go? What the fuck, man?"

"I didn't want you to come along for this," I mumble.

"You really fucking thought I'd just sit in my house in my fucking pajamas while you screw your whole life up?"

This goddamn loyalty of his is stronger than even my will.

I don't have a blood brother, but he's the closest thing I have to one.

The back door opens.

Finn and I startle and turn to look at the back.

A dark-haired man settles in. In the dim car light, his hair flashes a weird reddish-bronze and his light green eyes are disconcerting. "Evening Mr. Drevlow."

"You're—"

"The person you're supposed to meet. Brave, I must say. Hacking into our servers the way you did."

Finn glares at me.

I shrug at him. "It's your fault you got caught. What happened to your ultra-superior skills?"

"This is the fucking government we're talking about!"

The man in the back analyzes us with a detached but amused glance. "You're willing to get your hands dirty and you can get us the one person we're having a hard time getting to."

Because Barnard owes the Bratva so much money he's poured a considerable amount of what's left of his fortune into his own protection.

He's in hiding. Has been for the last few months. Does business from some hidden place. I'm sure Menahan knows where he is, but he won't be coughing him up.

Barnard just might be the only person in the world Menahan is actually loyal to.

But me? I can get him out. He wants me. Always has. He never got over what happened all those years ago, how his parents destroyed his life after I got him kicked out of school.

He wants me dead. When I offer myself up, he'll find a way to come knocking.

"What's your name?" Finn asks the man in the back.

The man gives him a dead smile. More a slight twisting of his lips really. "You both need clearance before you can get information like that."

"Clearance?"

"Just drive," the man says calmly. Someone used to having his orders obeyed. He settles back comfortably in the seat and stares out the window.

Finn and I exchange a look and I turn the ignition, wondering what the fuck we're about to get into.

Whatever it is, I don't give a fuck. I've already gone to hell for Lexi. I don't mind going deeper than that.

chapter 46

lexi
present

i didn't sleep for shit last night. It's 6:45am and I'm walking around my kitchen like a fucking zombie, lost in the chaos and mind-numbing need for respite.

I can't stop stressing about my mom.

Sadly—and much to my shame—that isn't the real reason I haven't slept.

Richard hates me. I know that now. His tone made it clear.

And why he hates me is eating at me. The questions. The unexpected pain.

I destroyed Drew once. Richard "won't let me do it again".

Stephen's drunken taunts echo in my head, telling me that I helped him more than anyone and didn't even know it. That his revenge against Drew was almost complete and it was all because of me.

My hands are shaking so hard I almost drop my mug full of coffee.

Drew let Kaylee record that video. He planned the whole thing to help his girl embarrass me, right? They had a twisted relationship. She would cheat on him and he had cheated on her. It's not so far-fetched that she agreed to let him do it.

All of them went down for it. Drew, Kaylee, Barnard, *and* Stephen. Barnard once told me the only reason he and Stephen went down is because Kaylee and Drew teamed up to blame them for it. That they were truly innocent.

All of them were kicked out of school days before graduation. Family money allowed them to still get their certificates and whatnot, but they couldn't attend the ceremony.

And all because of Drew.

Fuck. I'm back to calling him Drew?

Of course I am.

Because I'm starting to realize what an idiot I might be. There's more to what happened back then and I never dug deeper. I just let myself believe the worst about Andrew Drevlow because of who his father was.

But how could he be innocent? He *confessed*. Told the cops *and* the school board he was in on it.

He gave out names. Including his *girlfriend's* name.

Yet, Stephen's drunk, goading voice reaches out from the past, giving me nothing but doubt. *"Destroyed. Because of you. He was never going to survive not having you and now that's obvious."*

The newspaper headlines join in, adding to the mindfuck. Drew almost died a year-in-a-half after losing me. No one knows what caused the car wreck, but a few articles speculated that it was intentional.

Bile rises up my throat. Dear Lord, did he try to kill himself?

My phone starts vibrating against the counter with an incoming call. When I see the name across the screen, I snatch it up. "Hello?"

"Good morning Ms. Berkman. I wanted to take the time to call you personally."

"What's wrong Dr. Aaberg? What's happened to my mom?" One would think that, after years of this constant vigilance, of the brutal anxiety of waiting for the end, I would be used to this by now.

I'm not. My mom dying isn't an option for me. I'm nowhere near coming to terms with it.

"She did take a turn for the worse but we've stabilized her."

I exhale in relief.

"Her right lung collapsed last night—"

"*What*?" I almost screech.

"We inserted a chest tube to help with the leakage and pressure and she's fine now."

I start sobbing, the image of my mother having a tube inserted to help her breathe crushing me.

"Ms. Berkman, I'm actually calling with some good news."

"What could possibly be good news right now?"

"Your mother is being transferred."

"What?"

"Yes, we're prepping her to take her to Drevlow Systems, Inc. She'll be admitted to their pharmaceutical and medical division. They have one of the best—"

"Medical teams. I know. I work for them," I say numbly, in shock at what I'm hearing.

Dr. Aaberg is clearly in shock to hear I work for them. Then . . . "That explains it," he mumbles to himself.

"What?"

"You're her, aren't you?"

That question shatters the last of my world. Pieces of reality, of the story I'd believed, crumble at my feet. "Did . . . Did Andrew ask you to do this for my mother?"

"Yes. He was here visiting her last night when her lung collapsed."

My legs are the ones that almost collapse. I'm bombarded by relief, gratitude, suspicion, pain, questions. I don't have to wonder how he found out about my mom. The contract between his company and I states it very clear.

"Ye—years ago. When he almost died. Were you his attending physician?" I ask.

Dr. Aaberg hesitates. "Yes . . . But I can't tell you more than that. You'll have to ask Mr. Drevlow if you want that information."

He doesn't have to tell me anything else. *"You're her, aren't you?"*

"You almost killed him once; I will not allow you to get close to him and destroy him once again."

I grab onto the edge of the sink, shaking, on the verge of breaking apart. A sandcastle facing a hurricane. No chance of survival.

"I also want to let you know that Mr. Drevlow has hired me to be a part of your mom's medical team—"

"Because of your knowledge of her medical history *and* your connection with his family." I have no doubt of my claim. All it would take is a single hack, a break into the hospital's medical records, and I'd confirm it.

Dr. Aaberg has a long history with the Drevlow family.

He starts to deny the second part of my claim, clearly afraid of angering Drew by giving me too much information.

Fuck that. I'm getting the info myself. I bid Dr. Aaberg a good day and run out of my apartment. Destination? Work. I'm facing *my boss* today and demanding it all.

Even if the truth kills me.

chapter 47

lexi

present

My office is empty.

Empty.

My computers have been moved.

My—my *things*.

Oh God. Where are my pictures of my mom and I? *Where are they?*

I decided to stop down here before heading up and requesting a meeting with Andrew. Thought it would be nice to drop my purse off in my office.

But . . . this isn't my office anymore, is it?

It's not. The emptiness screams it at me.

What the fuck is going on?

"Ms. Berkman?"

I turn at the sound of that sweet, nervous voice and see a redhead standing behind me. *Megan.* She works down here, one of the lead software developers. Under me, of course. I was hired to be her boss.

Megan, with her 1950s style dresses, her cute short heels, and her navy blue, cat-eye glasses. Today her bright hair is in a ponytail high on her head.

She's eyeing me nervously. I adjust my own glasses and try to appear less unhinged. "Megan, do you have any idea—"

"Mr. Drevlow is waiting for you in his office. He wanted me to inform you to go straight up there."

Of course he is.

Pure, primal, commanding energy, forty-two floors above our heads, and I still feel him.

Waiting for me.

Calling me.

I felt him the moment I came down here.

"But my office—"

Megan swallows nervously. I realize she's intimidated by me now. When we met, most people seemed friendly and open enough.

Then Andrew stormed down here yesterday, bellowing my name like a conquering warlord seeking his plunder.

And just like that, he gave me power over these people. Power I didn't ask for.

"He said he'll explain everything to you."

I decide to take pity on the girl. She seems frightened enough as it is. Smiling, I nod. "Thanks for letting me know, Megan."

I step inside the elevator. Before I can even press the button for Andrew's floor, the doors close and the elevator begins ascending on it's own.

That's when I realize—this motherfucker is watching me in here. Clocking my every move. Commanding the elevator to rise up straight to him.

I turn and find the tiny orb of the camera on the ceiling. "I feel you, you bastard," I growl, glaring at it, not even caring that he might pick up on the meaning behind my confession.

What is he doing? First the thing with my mother, now this?

Why the hell is my office empty?

I'm not about to get fired. This I know deep in my core. In the same place I feel him, the sensation growing stronger with every floor the elevator climbs.

Suddenly, it stops and opens.

And just as suddenly, I'm afraid.

Before me is black marble floors. Black marble walls vined with gold. I don't know how far of a walk it is to his office—

Fuck that. I know. I know because of the maelstrom in the air, how close his presence feels.

And I'm scared out of my mind. Walking into that maelstrom . . . I'm not coming out of it the same. I'm not coming out of it my own person.

Andrew's intent is too bold in the air. As if the molecules themselves are warning me.

He plans to own you.

Ridiculous thought. I must be paranoid. It can't be true.

It is, my mind insists.

But what choice do I have? I have to go in there.

So I do. My heels click on the marble with every nervous step. I only take three when I realize that there's a glass wall to my left.

Behind that glass wall? The vast expanse of the Drevlow throne. A high-tech, black marble, gold, and glass gilded power center, with it's king leaning against his massive desk, facing me.

I'm lightheaded. Panicky. It's isn't until Andrew shifts off that desk, a deadly predator in a dark suit uncoiling, that I realize why.

I stopped breathing.

Toffee colored bedroom eyes stare at me, unflinching, cataloging every weakness.

Whatever truly happened all those years ago, this man plans to own me.

And he isn't going to give me a choice in the matter.

He approaches the glass wall and a part of it slides open automatically.

That's when I notice the large desk to my left, directly in front of the wall. It's huge.

Well, it has to be. It's holding four monitor screens and *all my shit* on top of it. "Wh—what is this?" I whisper, my pulse a thunderous, weakening storm in my veins. I'm too out of breath to even speak properly.

"It's your new desk, Lexi." So calm and yet so turbulent at the same time. That gaze ineffable, and universal, and all-consuming like a supernova collapsing into a black hole.

"What?" I whisper, shaking all over. Dear God, what's wrong with me? What is *this*?

My pulse pounds hardest between my legs, screaming out the truth.

The madness of this hunger is something I almost forgot. Almost. After everything I went through and what Stephen did to me, I went numb. Couldn't feel. It afforded me a cushion. A way to almost erase the memory of this insanity.

Andrew draws closer and it occurs to me that he can sense *me*. That he knows what's happening to me and he's actually trying to not frighten me anymore. "It's your new desk," he repeats softly.

It's that soft tone that almost does me in. The tenderness that tinges his wild need for me. "Isn't that where your assistant . . . sits?" I finish the last part on yet another whisper, my eyes widening with realization.

"Yes, Lexi. You've been promoted. You'll be working from here from now on."

chapter 48

andrew

present

my entire body pulses with bright violent images of me backing Lexi up and lifting her onto that desk.

I'm so amped, so on fire, that all it'd take is three nice strokes to explode inside her. Three hard, deep strokes.

She's right there with me. Her lush little body shakes with desire, and I know she'd come all over my dick.

You can't. She's fragile. And I have no facts, only a brutal suspicion that makes me wilder.

It shouldn't. It should make me softer. More caring. It should give me the power to treat her carefully.

But the thought of anyone hurting that sexy body of hers only makes me want it more. I'll please her. Destroy her. Make her come so many times her mind will shatter from the pleasure.

She'll never be right again.

No. She won't. And that's how I'll know she is finally mine again.

"Your assistant?" she asks, and I can't fault her for the way her tone trembles with fear.

You should be afraid, baby. You should be out of your mind with your need to escape. I'm wired to take everything from you. To make you a puppet on my string. I'm *made* to own you like you're the most precious thing in my entire fucking universe and we both know I'm not going to be able to stop myself.

"Yes," I say simply, arms crossed, like my mind isn't a malfunctioning mess of primal impulses.

"But . . . I'm supposed to be on the Providence project—" Her excuse is weak and feeble, even to her own ears.

"You will. You'll be coordinating the entire team and working alongside me. But—"

"I'll also be working as your assistant. Your *personal* assistant." There. A spark of sexy defiance in her eyes. The type that revs me the fuck up. Excites me like nothing else.

I want her surrender.

I'm going to have it.

But I want to have the scars of her all over me when I win. I want her to add to the marks already left on my body by the loss of her.

I can't help but smile at her. Lexi sucks her breath in sharply at the sight of my smile. Running my hand across my lips, I remind myself I need to find civility somewhere. My woman was probably hurt in ways I don't yet understand. I can't go off like a wild man on her.

"Come. You'll be training directly inside with me for the next few days." An extra chair is already placed beside my desk.

"No," she snaps, fear finally transforming into defiance.

I walk into my office anyway, smiling. She'll follow. She has no

TWISTED HEARTBREAK

choice. I saw the questions in her eyes. She wants things from me and she knows the only way to get them is by being close to me.

I'm already by my desk when I feel her behind me. What I don't expect is for her to spin me around.

She pushes me back against my desk and glares up at me.

I let my eyes caress her, knowing that I'm a fool for doing so. That focusing on her for too long is nothing more than a tease to my starved heart.

Her hair is wavy on the ends today, like she didn't have enough time to straighten it out.

Those big, luscious curls are still there. I vow to myself that one day I'll see them again.

"Tell me exactly what happened seven years ago." Her voice wavers, and I hear the fragility of her so damn clearly.

Whatever happened to her all these years, her hate of me helped keep her strong. Gave her something to focus on. If I tell her the truth, I'll be taking that away from her.

"Tell me what Menahan did to you, Lexi," I counter softly, hands fisted at my sides to stop myself from touching her.

Her teary eyes blink in surprise—I see the deception fall over them like a shade, before she even speaks. "He infected my mother to keep me under his control."

Half a truth.

Enough to detonate the last of my humanity.

I feel the darkness fully unleash itself in my veins, but I focus on Lexi's eyes instead of giving away the sudden bloodlust taking over me. "What else did he do?" I ask softly, slowly.

Lexi shakes her head, backing away from me, striving for cool denial.

Even as her trembling increases and the stark despair of trauma overflows her eyes.

And, in that moment, without uttering a single word to me, she conveys the very thing I'd been suppressing.

That twisted suspicion.

Had it not been true, I could've been saved me from becoming a true villain.

I can barely breathe as I finally admit to myself what deep down I'd already known.

Stephen Menahan raped my woman.

chapter 49

andrew
present

turns out, not even the government is all powerful.

Well, it can be, but when dealing with the lives of their undercover agents and all the intel—read: usefulness—that those people can provide, even the government has to play within a certain set of rules.

No outward involvement until the operation is finished.

Everything has to be done stealth. Sneaky.

And they don't give a damn who dies because of it. Not when going up against their most bitter enemies.

The man struggling in the dark right now, tied to that chair, has done nothing to warrant the government's ire.

He's just a means to an end for them. Expendable.

A perfect tool to get their guy even more of a foothold within the mafia.

I heard a well-orchestrated lie once. That the government doesn't condone their agents getting deeply involved with the criminal activities of their targets. Especially the killing.

A well-orchestrated, well marketed lie, as I said. Maybe that's how it works with the FBI. Hell, maybe that's how it even works with the CIA.

But whatever branch of the government sent that bronze-haired motherfucker into the Bratva, they *want* him deeply involved with every aspect of their trade.

Especially the killing.

I've been sitting in the dark, in the same stone cellar as my victim, for two hours now.

Two hours ago, the undercover sat me down in another room outside of here and asked me if I understood what I'm getting myself into. Offered to do the killing for me.

Here's the thing. He doesn't have to prove to anyone he killed the piece of shit I hear gasping in front of me. He just has to produce the body.

I declined his offer.

It's a deal between me and him. His bosses don't know about it. Why he's obliging me I'll never know.

Maybe he senses that, no matter how much of a professional he is and how much more training than me he has, there's nothing in the world that can stop me.

The soon-to-be dead man in front of me takes a deep breath and resumes his struggles. "Hello?" he screams into the darkness. "Is anyone out there? We can talk this out! I have the money ready in my offshore account!"

Too fucking late.

He left the Bratva waiting too long. Went into hiding. Now it's a matter of reputation. He has to die for trying to play them like fools.

And even if that weren't the case, now he has to deal with *me*.

I wonder if somewhere deep inside his primitive, lizard brain he senses the seconds ticking away, counting down to his last breath.

He screams out for someone again.

I slowly take a cigarette out of the box I bought earlier. I haven't smoked in years. Ever since I went through rehab. A junkie should avoid all addictions. Dipping into just one of them could mean a downward spiral back into the pit.

Too bad I'm already halfway there and too consumed with my need to kill to stop myself. "No one's coming for you."

He stops struggling, stunned into silence at the sound of my voice. The only sound for a few seconds is his panicked, quick breaths.

That's right. He knows. He has more to fear from me than the Bratva.

And to think. The moment I called him, faking desperation, confessing I knew what Menahan did to my Lexi, *begging* to see him so I could convince him to help me, he thought he had his chance.

I agreed to meet him in a closed down warehouse lot, at 1:00am, for "old times' sake."

He thought that, in my desperation, I was fooled. That I believed he'd actually help me go up against his best friend.

He also thought he could come with two of his men and finally take me out.

See, that's the difference between him and Menahan. They can both hold a grudge for eternity and it makes them thirsty for blood.

Menahan is smart about it. Logical.

This waste of skin is impulsive. Emotional.

He still despises me for getting him kicked out of school. His strict, abusive dad sent him to military school until he was twenty-two. From what I understand, it wasn't the typical military school. Fucked up shit was done to him there.

Funny, not even that could teach him self-control and patience.

And he blames me for all his trauma, of course.

That's okay. I hold him partially to blame for everything me and my girl went through the last seven years.

Putting the cigarette to my lips, I calmly flick the lighter, and hold the flame right at the end of it.

Letting Barnard see my face illuminated in the dim light.

He's sweaty. Pupils blown from both fear and the dark.

I still remember the look in my father's eyes when my words caused him that final heart attack. When it first started, I saw the truth shining in them. The realization that it was over.

A dead man's look.

It's the same look on Barnard's face right now. The look of a man that knows his time is up.

I light the cigarette and take a pull. After years of not smoking, a person is supposed to struggle with the first few pulls, lungs going into a mini-shock from the bombardment of smoke.

I take to it like I never left. Like the black tar I'm inhaling was always meant to be a part of me even if I took a years-long break from it.

When I killed my father by telling him what I did, I felt calm. Unemotional in the sense of purpose. I wanted him dead but I also knew he had to go, and that it had to be by my hand.

I guess smoking and killing go hand-in-hand for people like me. I feel the same way about Barnard's imminent death as I do about the cigarette. As I did about my father dying.

As if this was just a role I was always meant to step into.

Torturer.

Murderer.

I palm the little remote in my hand and press the button, sending all the lights blazing on.

The pathetic sycophant in front of me reeks of fear. Desperation. Real shit, not faked.

TWISTED HEARTBREAK

"I—I had nothing to do with him raping her—"

I lean back in my seat calmly, as if the mention of that doesn't threaten to send me flying at him, teeth bared for his throat.

"You're truly one of the only things he cares about," I say, flicking the ash off my cigarette.

"And Lexi. He truly loves her. He didn't mean to—"

Wrong. Thing. To. Say.

I press another button and a side of the wall next to us slides up. Behind it is a cage.

Inside that cage is four rabid dogs, massive in size.

They, like me, smell Barnard's fear in the air and it awakens their killer instincts.

Barnard takes one look at them and pisses his fucking pants.

The acrid smell of his urine is like an appetizer to the angry mutts. They hurl themselves up against the cage, massive jaws snapping.

"This is what they said they would do to you when they found you, no?" I raise my eyebrows nonchalantly, waiting for a response.

"Andrew, *please* man. We were like brothers once—"

I interrupt him yet again. This time by calmly standing. "And then you humiliated my woman. Caused me to lose her. Helped Stephen hide, control, and abuse her. I'll make sure to send him one of your body parts as a gift once it's over." I mean that, too.

Turning, I walk out the room, ignoring Barnard's desperate screams for help. For forgiveness. For every damn thing my girl and I weren't afforded the last seven years.

The heavy metal door closes behind me. Without even looking back at it, I press the button to open the cage.

The sound of Barnard's horrified scream as the dogs come at him follows me down the hall.

BOOK ONE

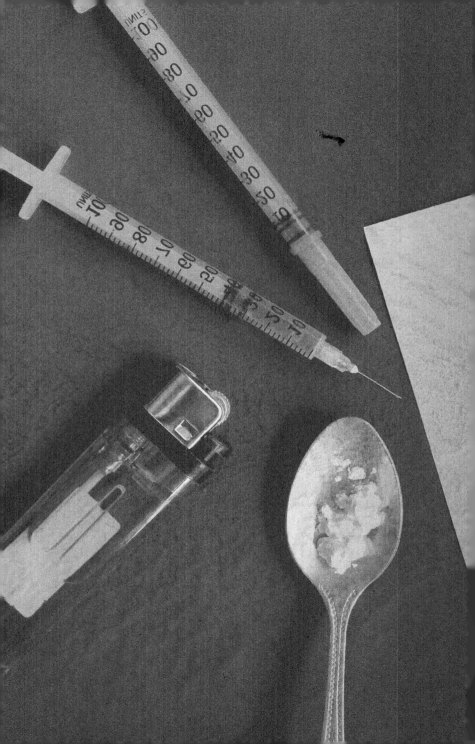

chapter 50

<u>andrew</u>
7 years ago

there's a small window above my head. The sun started shining through a while ago. Has to have been three hours, at least.

I've been sitting on this cot the whole time.

The lighting is naturally dim back here. I can see dust particles flying inside the bright ray of sun pouring in.

That's all I've have to focus on. That and the growing black hole in my fucking gut.

Overnight. That's how long they've kept me in this fucking cell. Me. A Drevlow.

But that's exactly why I've been here this long. Because my father, Mr. Drevlow, demanded that I stay here and "learn my lesson".

He knows I took the blame.

Fuck. *I took the blame.*

I lean forward, elbows braced on my knees, and run my hand

over my buzz-cut hair. Everything's shaking. My leg is bouncing.

All I can imagine is Lexi out there, suffering. Thinking God knows what.

In my defense, at the time I believed I would be out of here in two hours, tops. Not that I'd be here until the next day.

The logic was simple: I was going to take the blame. All of us would pay for whatever pain my girl is going through.

And I was going to have enough time to get to her, explain my goal.

As long as the cops believe I was in on the whole recording scheme, I can make it seem more legit when we're all brought before the school board.

There's no doubt. We will be. This entire ordeal goes against the very stringent rules set forth by the board.

I don't give a fuck that this will get me thrown out of school— actually, I'm banking on it.

I'm taking all those motherfuckers with me when I go.

By now, my father knows I said I was in on this. He should've been proud. Ecstatic that I hurt Berkman's daughter.

The fact that he left me here overnight and sent me that little message via my lawyer can only mean one thing.

My father knows I'm lying.

Either Kaylee got to him and told him the truth . . .

Or I couldn't convince him that I'd changed my mind about wanting Lexi. Couldn't undo my mistake of telling him I wanted to be with her.

"Fuck. Fuck. Fuck." I haven't slept. Can't. Has nothing to do with being in this cell.

Everything feels wrong. I don't know how to explain it. Like there's some telepathic connection between Lexi and I.

It's almost like I can *feel* everything she's feeling. Can feel how the damage sinks in deeper with every moment that she's out there without me.

I have to get to her. Have to explain . . .

"Daddy said you can finally go, tough shot."

The sound of keys, more than that asshole's taunts, brings me back to reality. I'm on my feet before he's done opening the gate.

My lawyer is standing just outside the holding area. He steps toward me as I barrel out, his mouth open to speak.

"Not now." I storm past him.

He's calling my name. Chasing after me. Ignoring him, I head straight to the door—

My father steps inside, his back straight. Bearing impeccable in his ridiculously expensive suit.

He's standing right in front of the door, blocking my way. I hope for his sake he gets the hint when I don't slow down and he moves.

Of course, he doesn't.

He reaches out to grab my arms as I approach. The look on his face is one I know well.

He's ready to lay down his law with me.

"Where do you think you're going?" He grabs my arms.

I tell him once, calmly, "Let me go."

"Where do you think you're going?" he repeats.

"I said, let me go!" I yell, shoving him out of my way with all my strength. Several voices yell out behind me as I barge out the door.

There's no stopping to take in the fact that I finally got to push my father. Give him some of the aggression I've been choking on for so long.

No stopping to be ashamed at my thoughts either.

Shit. *Shit.* I don't have my car here with me. Obviously, my father isn't going to let me take his car to get back to Lexi.

Fuck it. I'll run.

chapter 51

lexi
present
17 hours before barnard wellington's disappearance

"*What else did he do?*"

Hell. I think I'm still shaking my head. Forcing myself to stop, I somehow find the strength to look at him.

Pretending I'm not lying.

That I'm not panicking.

What about me gave it away? What? *Damn it.*

"You can't force me to work up here with you, Andrew."

Just minutes ago, he was treading carefully with me. Trying not to scare me.

My words drag something different out of him. Gone is the soothing, cautious Andrew. A hardness falls over him, the kind of unrelenting energy that signals his indomitable will.

"Lexi. You're under contract. I'm your boss. And I need you up here."

My lips fall open at his audacity. At the calm way he stated that. "You're really going there?"

"You and I have an enemy in common, Ms. Berkman. I need you to become my right hand in order for us to succeed."

"*I hate you*," I say, blinking in disbelief. "How could you want me to be your right hand?"

"And I—" He inhales deeply instead of finishing what he was going to say.

"You what?"

Shaking his head, Andrew leans back on his desk and crosses his arms; the exact same pose he was in when I first approached the glass wall. "I'm your boss and I'm telling you I need you here."

"I need to be able to coordinate the team. Paul. Megan—"

"She's been promoted to your position. You'll be coordinating the team from up here."

My face burns hot with frustration. With the futility suddenly creeping in on me. I remember this feeling of having my choices taken away from me by a prick with too much power.

"I'm the best fucking coder in this entire building, Drew." Once again, that freaking nickname leaves my mouth before I realize it.

Andrew's expression softens. "I *know*, Lexi. And I'm not too shabby myself."

I know. I remember. He was a genius back then, I can only imagine how dangerous that mind is now.

Still. "You aren't better than me."

He nods. "No I'm not. But together, we'd be dangerous and you know it."

Deep down, I know he's right. The logic is irrefutable. Bringing down Menahan isn't just about releasing a headset superior to his. Undermining his company by taking top spot.

It's about finding ways into his systems. Getting the information we need to best him.

The devil fuck me, but I'll be helping the Drevlow name grow with that outcome.

But as long as my mother gets the help she needs out of this, what else can I do?

"You're starting to see my logic, aren't you?"

Fucking asshole.

Fisting my hands, I look around the office. My new workplace. "I'll only agree to work up here on one condition."

"Shoot."

Huffing out a sarcastic laugh, I turn back to him. "You confessed to the cops." I saw the video. His father made it his mission to come show me.

And then he offered me that bargain, and I was stupid enough to take it.

Stupid enough to send myself down such a horrid path.

"I did." Andrew stares into my eyes.

Swallowing, I blink back tears. "So you admit you betrayed me." What am I expecting, a different answer? I saw the video for myself!

His head tilts back and his expression turns defiant. "I'll tell you the exact details of what happened back then—"

"So it was more than that?" Was that a hint of desperation I heard in my tone?

"—if you tell me what happened between you and Stephen. *All* of it."

Why does he keep asking me?

Obviously, I know. I did something that gave it away. Andrew suspects Stephen abused me much more than I'm letting on.

I'll never let him know. I can't. All these years, it was about getting away. Every step calculated. Planned. I needed to escape Stephen's hold and that was all I could focus on.

I've just rediscovered sexual pleasure at the hands of the man before me.

Dealing with what happened to me, though? No. I haven't even begun processing that fully.

How the hell am I even supposed to?

And Andrew expects me to share it? *Out of his mind.* It feels too private. Too . . . too . . . "You know what? Forget this." I turn to leave.

"*Please.*"

My heart crumbles painfully. I pause mid-step, pressing a hand to my chest. Why is it hurting so much?

"Lexi, please."

I spin to face Drew again, dropping my hand.

He's still in the same position I left him, but his eyes . . .

God help me, I'm in so much pain right now.

"Being up here is going to be hard," I confess, my tone weaker than it should be.

His eyes somehow soften even more. "I know."

"Then why are you doing this?"

"Because I honestly have no choice."

chapter 52

lexi
present
10 hours before barnard wellington's disappearance

What does he mean by that?

I search his eyes, his beautiful eyes—

Holy crap. I didn't just think that.

But I did.

"Be logical about this," he urges in that flat tone, as if *he's* the one being logical.

Yes. Strategically it's the best move. When it comes to destroying Stephen that is.

Out of nowhere, the lock I keep tight on my memories fails, and I'm reminded of *why* Stephen needs to be destroyed.

"Stephen! Please! What are you doing?"

"It's mine, Lexi. It's always been mine. Just like that pussy."

Pain tears my insides, radiating out from my ass, like a knife stabbing deep.

It hurts. Oh God, save me. It hurts.

"Lexi? Lexi!"

I blink.

Then I jump back, breathing hard.

Andrew's right in front of me. He fists his hands, veins bulging, but makes no move to follow me.

He knows I can't handle that right now.

Panting, I tear my stare away from him. Holy hell, why the fuck? But I know why. It isn't the first time one of the memories come at me without warning.

I've gotten good at holding them back. I can go weeks now without getting lost in the recollections. Regardless of what my therapist believes, I know that I will come to completely suppress those memories with time.

I *will* forget.

I have to.

"*Lexi.*"

That pained groan centers me. If I weren't so freaked out about almost losing myself to that panic, it would register that he's my lifeline at this moment.

Somehow, his obvious pain over seeing my own gives me the strength to withhold the anxiety.

But I don't analyze that. "You're right." I resist the urge to run my shaking hand across my mouth. "To destroy him, we need to be a team. Our planning has to be perfect."

Because this is my reality and I can't allow any weakness to affect that.

Andrew Drevlow is my enemy, but he never, ever did to me any of the things Stephen has done.

"Lexi . . ."

"But I will not talk about anything other than our plans to bring him down and work with you." My voice shakes with the warning.

His jaw muscle pumps; he always had a bad habit of grinding his teeth when stressed. "Fine. Your rules."

I'm shocked by his easy acquiescence. Like hell it's *my* rules. I know him. He was never the type of guy to let anyone take the reins.

The furious light in his eyes tells me he isn't too keen on letting me take them now.

"Why?" I ask him, raising my chin. Why are you giving in so easy? Why are you actually *respecting* my desires?

He lowers his chin and stares me deep in the eye. "You. Know. Why."

I shake my head. I don't.

He exhales, nostrils flaring softly, and his fists finally unclench. "The first thing I need you to do is hire yourself an assistant."

My eyebrows rise at that.

"You're too important to be bogged down with mundane things like answering my calls and keeping track of my calendar."

"You should have thought about that before strong-arming me into the role."

Andrew stops for a second, his expression unreadable.

When his lips twitch and his expression melts with affection, I swear I feel the ground beneath my heels shift. "God. I missed your stubborn comebacks."

No.

No.

My body steps away from him, a single step, but my head's also shaking and I see the moment he catches on to my fear.

Please. Please don't make me feel this again. Not with you.

I swear I can hear his voice in my head. *You never stopped, Lexi.*

I can't do this. Can't be near this man. I'm not strong enough. What the hell was I thinking?

The intercom on Andrew's desk beeps right before a woman's voice comes through. "Mr. Drevlow. I have your 9:00am here to see you."

I would love to say the spell is broken.

For me, it's not.

What the fuck is wrong with me?

Andrew half turns to press the answering button. "Let him up."

I'm already backing away, seeing my small way out.

"Wait."

I pause by the glass wall.

"Delegate whatever you have to. I'm giving you full control as my right hand."

Me? *Me*? The world is upside down. Twisted. Me as the right hand to the head of the *Drevlow* empire?

Immeasurable power.

Tainted privilege.

This empire crushed the likes of my father and now I'm going to help run it? Not just help it grow, but actually steer a portion of it? Command it?

Use it against Stephen. I feel poisoned at the thought of what I must do, but this has been my life for almost a decade, I remind myself.

A puppet of powerful men. A puppet of cruel fate. I learned to deal. To survive. To use everything to my advantage.

No need to stop now.

"Fine," I tell him, heading straight for my desk.

chapter 53

lexi

present

16 hours before barnard wellington's disappearance

by the time Andrew's 9:00am gets off the elevator a minute or so later, I'm calmer.

I think.

I've busied myself firing up both desktops on my desk. Arranging my frames and knickknacks can be done later. I'm all about business right now. Setting up the most important aspects so Andrew and I can move forward with our plan.

The man he's meeting walks in, flashing me a bright white smile once he sees me. He's fairly handsome with his tanned skin, and everything about him screams *money*.

Andrew's already at the glass wall, waiting for him. "Asad. Come in." His tone is terse and I get the feeling that he doesn't like how *Asad* just smiled at me.

Asad turns that smile Andrew's way as he greets him. But when he walks by my desk, his eyes cut in my direction again and I freeze.

His eyes. That look . . .

I've seen it before.

Stephen.

A cold shiver rips down my spine.

"Considering you need me to agree to this contract, let's start things off on the right foot. Shall we?" Andrew's voice is deadly soft.

Deadly serious.

I sneak a glance at him and my heart drops at the dark light in *his* eyes.

There it is again. That madness.

For some reason, it scares me more than what I saw in Asad's gaze. Than the memory of Stephen.

It's the first time the question crosses my mind, but I can't help but mentally ask him, *What have you become?*

I know the answer to that. I've dealt with enough evil to recognize it when I see it.

"Of course. What do you need?" Asad stops before Andrew and offers his hand to shake.

Andrew doesn't even stare at it. "You don't look at her. You don't think about her. And for your sake, you don't dare to even *dream* about her."

I can't help my gasp at that.

Asad looks between both of us, his eyebrows rising with amusement. "I thought she was just another employee—"

"She's not."

"So she's yours then?"

I bristle at that and my mouth flies open to deny it.

"It goes beyond that," is Andrew's serious response.

I swear to God, I almost fall off this chair.

Did he . . . did this asshole just claim me?

Asad waves a hand dismissively, expression good-natured.

"Point taken. As I said, I didn't know." He doesn't seem phased by the threat pouring off Andrew. Motioning with his head to Drew's office, he says, "Shall we proceed?"

And with that, they both walk inside, the glass wall automatically sliding shut behind them.

I can't rip my eyes away from Andrew. Fury strangles me. Helplessness.

Terror.

He wants to own me just as much as Stephen did.

He's the only man capable of giving me pleasure.

No matter what Stephen did, he never owned me. He broke me. Trapped me. Choked me with the far reach of his leash, but I never let him in.

Andrew . . .

He's been there. Is still there. I was never able to purge this demon out of me. Never able to bleed him out.

And I bled. God help me, I *bled.*

I decide to focus on the anger because thinking about anything else will break my already cracked mind. Once his meeting is over, I'm going to force him to understand.

I'm not his. Fuck what my body has to say about it, I have my free will. I fought hard to break free of Stephen so I could exercise it again, and I'll be damned if Andrew comes along and tries to take that from me.

Turning back to my screen, I busy myself contacting the HR department and asking them to start a search for an assistant. I make it clear that I need to have someone hired by tomorrow, latest.

Yes. I know. It's short notice, but there's no time. The faster we bring down Stephen, the faster I can escape Andrew.

He'll never let you go.

I break out in a cold sweat.

Ignoring it, I log onto my personal email, making sure to encrypt the connection.

There's an unread email at the very top of my inbox. One that ends my entire world.

I know that email address anywhere. Of course I would.

SMenahan@Menahanindustries.com

Don't open it. Ignore it. It's not the first time he's reached out to me since I left. Not the first email or text.

And like every single time, the sick curiosity cannot be fought. I click open the email, shaking . . .

I knew you love me. I'm so grateful for your surprise.

What the fuck?

You're finally in. Just imagine baby. We can finally destroy him once and for all. Then we can go back to being together.

He's sick. So sick–

A hand lands next to me on the desk and I jump, chair skidding back.

It's Andrew, and that homicidal glint is expanding in his eyes, overcoming his facial expression.

He's reading the email.

I scramble to grab my mouse and shut the computer down.

He grabs the mouse from me and yanks the keyboard closer.

And before I know it, he's begun typing out a response.

chapter 54

andrew

7 years ago

i'm in phenomenal fucking shape, but even I'm dying as I approach Lexi's street. The precinct is four miles away. It took me way longer than it should have to get here.

Damn my human legs.

My heart is failing in my chest, the pressure of the run getting to me.

But it isn't just that. I know it isn't. Something is wrong and the closer I get to her house, I can feel it.

I hang onto the hope of seeing her face. Of explaining. Of getting through to her.

I pray that somehow she hasn't heard that I took the blame. All I want to do is buffer her. Explain my lie and what I'm hoping to get out of it.

My body starts slowing, and I'm choking for breath.

But my feet hit the pavement on the corner and I can see the two-story, white structure from here.

I burst back into a run, full speed, Lexi's face all I can see. Her lips all I want. Her in my arms all I need.

I'm halfway down the block when I see it.

The "For Sale" sign impaled on the front yard.

I slam to a halt and my speed sends me skidding onto the street, my knees scraping through my jeans on impact.

I don't even feel it.

Wh—what the fuck . . . No. That's impossible. My eyes rise, taking in the entire house . . .

Everything's dark. The house seems empty.

No. It isn't. They live here. I just dropped Lexi off two nights ago.

I'm useless, trembling with a weakness I've never felt before. It takes me two tries to get to my feet, and my legs are shaking to the point that I almost can't stay upright.

A car pulls up next to me. "Andrew! Man, I heard you were out. Listen—"

Finn.

I'm already walking away from him, deadened feet stepping onto the curb.

Somehow, that single step echoes in me. All around me. A deafening sound that confuses me. Something just happened. I don't know what, but everything is changing around me.

My life is never going to be the same again and I can *feel* the shift in my destiny.

Fear begs me to stop. Cease moving. Take a moment to reorient myself. To come to terms with the pieces of my life that are melting away.

"Drew! Stop, man. We have to talk."

TWISTED HEARTBREAK

I start running again, like a possessed bullet aimed at the house, and I'm on the porch in seconds.

The porch swing is missing. The windchime that was hanging above the door. Potted plants. Welcome mat.

I drove by here after dropping her off to make sure she got inside. I remember seeing all those things.

"No. No. No." I don't even realize those frantic grunts are coming from me. Behind me, Finn calls out my name again and I hear the sound of running footsteps. Stumbling over my own feet, I approach the window.

No shades. Darkness on the other side. Emptiness.

A chasm breaks open inside me, a crack that quickly spreads. *Shit. Something's broken.* I have enough semblance of mind to know how illogical the thought is. I'm still standing. Still breathing. Organs still functioning. Yet I hear my own voice in my head, behind the roar of my heart, begging for mercy.

To be saved.

Finn lands on the porch behind me. Detached, I take in the frightened, worried way he's staring at me. "Andrew. Stop for a second, okay?" His voice is shaky.

Do I look that bad?

Numb, that voice still begging in my head, I nudge him out of the way and approach the front door. I stop in front of it.

And that's when he says it. "Lexi's gone, Drew."

A loud, enraged sound reaches my ears—my foot connects with the door, sending it flying inward, flakes of wood raining down.

"Drew!"

I storm into the house.

The utterly empty house.

Finn's words repeat themselves in my mind again. *"Lexi's gone, Drew."* That sound again. That loud roar.

It's me. As I drop down to my knees, my head snaps back, my

BOOK ONE

mouth opening to let loose an animalistic shout. Like a spectator seeing myself from afar, I can only watch in horror as my humanity is stripped from me and I become nothing more than an injured beast.

God, what is this? What the fuck is happening to me?

Stupid question. I know what this is. I've been building up to this moment my entire, miserable life.

The shattered boy has finally snapped.

It's fine, I tell myself. *It's fine. You'll find her. Don't fucking overreact to this.*

I won't find her. Somehow, I know this in my fucking bones.

Suddenly, the proof of it walks through the door. "Enough with the hysterics, son. She's gone. Now get up before the cops arrive. There's no doubt the neighbors called them."

My head snaps around to him, I manage to growl out a single word—"*You*"—and then I'm off my feet, my sneakers pounding into the floor.

He did this. Him. I know he did. He's the reason she's gone. *HIM.*

After everything he's done to me. All the things he's taken from me.

My father has a split second to realize I'm coming at him full-throttle—

We crash through the broken doorway, straight out onto the porch.

chapter 55

lexi

present

16 hours before barnard wellington's disappearance

"What the fuck are you doing?" I whisper angrily, acutely aware that Asad's eyes are on us. I almost reach out to yank Andrew's arm, pull him away from the keyboard, but remind myself that touching him isn't worth the risk.

I'm quivering at the feel of his body heat mere inches from me. "*Andrew.*" My voice catches as I focus on the response he's typing out.

Your days of contacting her are done. Reach out to her again, and I'll make sure the whole world finds out what you've done to her.

"Stop," I beg in a reedy whisper. "What are you thinking—"

He hits send.

And just like that, another part of my personal life is taken from me, yet another thing no longer under my control.

Even worse, Andrew's response kills any lingering iota of doubt I had.

That man knows Stephen raped me.

My personal email has become yet another battleground in the war between these two men.

Stephen sends a reply almost immediately. *We were together. That's all it was. She wanted me and I wanted her. Tell me, does she know what you've been up to all these years?*

What?

"Is everything alright?" Asad is standing at the glass wall, his eyes alit with morbid curiosity.

He likes this, I notice. This man is envious of Drew for some reason and he's loving watching him lose his composure.

I, on the other hand, am trapped in a losing tug-a-war with impulse. My eyes flicker to Andrew, and all I want to do is get him alone and find out the truth.

What did you do?

What is Stephen talking about?

God damn it. If we're going to be partners, he has to be open with me about all of his moves. Strategically, this isn't going to work unless we keep each other informed.

I tell myself that's the only reason for my desperation to know.

Andrew straightens away from my desk and smoothes his hand down his blazer. "We've been handling some lowlives trying to hack into our servers for a while."

He sounds so calm. As if he didn't just threaten Stephen-fucking-Menahan through my personal email account.

As if he didn't just imply that he's going to let an entire world know I was sexually abused.

Over my dead body, I think, fury rising. How could he do this to me? So, he knows what I've been through. No details, of course, but he knows, and he's willing to air my shame before an entire world?

Horrid headlines flash in my mind as I imagine the public scandal.

I agreed to bring Stephen down, but not like this.

"Ah. So you need to double check that your assistant's email is safe." Asad's sarcastic disbelief is plainly evident, even though his tone is calm and understanding.

Andrew stops before him, expression flat. "Ms. Berkman isn't my office assistant. She's the lead programmer for the entire company."

Another hit.

Another unexpected twist.

With sudden trepidation, I realize that this man has me *reeling*. Too fast. Everything's happening too fast. I can't keep up.

Just like before with him. Exactly like before. Nothing but a roller coaster moving at lightspeed.

"Your most valuable asset, then." Asad's interest in me seems to have ramped up to a ridiculous degree.

"Yes. *Mine*. Now do me a favor and get in the office so we can finish this. I have other important things to handle today."

My God. Andrew's arrogance is on an entire other level. He has no qualms about talking to Asad as if he's nothing.

Asad, however, laughs. As if it's no big deal. "You are ruthless. I knew that the moment I met you, but even I am impressed."

Andrew says nothing, waiting for Asad to walk back into the office. His head turns in my direction, his eyes soft.

Is he silently fucking apologizing to me right now?

Christ help me, this man has me all kinds of twisted, confused, and scrambled.

He sends me one more look and the message in his eyes is clear: *tell me if he contacts you again.*

I continue glaring at him. Once he's turned his back and the glass has slid shut, I drag my keyboard to me, close down my email, and pretend I'm just getting back to work.

In reality, I'm working my way into the company's main servers, into the employee files. It takes me less than five minutes to get all the info I need.

To my annoyance, there's no personal information on Andrew. The only near personal thing I find is his cell.

I grab mine and type out a text.

Lexi: No more bullshit. As soon as he's out of there, we need to talk.

This conversation might end up doing me more harm than good, but it's time it fucking happens. That man has to understand that he doesn't call the shots here, I do, and he isn't going to force me back onto his fucked-up ride.

I can't allow it.

chapter 56

lexi

present

15 hours before barnard wellington's disappearance

by the time Asad leaves, I'm elbow-deep into lines upon lines of coding. Paul emailed the file to me over an hour ago. On top of that, HR took my request very—and I do mean, *very*—seriously. There's already ten resumes of potential candidates for me to go through.

I've dubbed the effect, *"The roar heard around the world."* Or this building, to be exact. I haven't even stepped into any kind of position of power here, and one man screaming my name already has people scrambling to please me.

Ah, but that's the Drevlow syndrome, isn't it? There's something about the men of that family that sets them apart. Something so off in their very DNA, that other people can sense it. Be wary of it.

Everyone's afraid of those monsters.

I wonder exactly what Andrew did to prove to his employees,

in such a short amount of time, that he's also a force to be reckoned with.

Then again, have you seen him? Everything about that man screams, *I will destroy you. Get in the way of what I want, and it'll be the end of you.*

It was always that way, but now, this new version of him . . .

I push it out of my mind. It's none of my fucking business what Andrew Drevlow has gone through, what it did to him, and if he's still warped by any of it.

He's clearly still warped. Yeah, I saw it. Recognized the look in his eyes. I've been seeing it in the mirror my whole life, ever since *his* father drove mine to suicide. And the last few years, stuck under Stephen's control?

Whatever. I can't keep thinking about this. I've come here to accomplish two goals:

Get my mother the help she needs.

Destroy Stephen.

Everything else is irrelevant.

I'm so absorbed in my thoughts, I nearly miss Asad's departure.

But that's the thing about negative-conditioning. Once it sets in, it buries deep into your subconscious, corroding your instinctual responses.

I spent years in the sights of a twisted predator. My skin seems to have evolved a sensory system, a way to warn me when I'm being sized up. Skin going cold, I look up from my screen.

Asad walks by my desk on his way to the elevators. Those darks eyes violate me. Undress me. With a single look, his given away what he's doing to me in his mind.

There's nothing hot or sexy about it. This man isn't just imagining that he's fucking me. In his fantasies, he's *breaking* me.

I feel abused all over again.

He steps into the elevator, and just like that, he's gone.

I still can't breathe right.

"He even so much as looks your way again . . ."

I jump in my seat, my head flying around.

Andrew's standing at the open glass wall, expression stoic, eyes brimming with that sick evil I saw before. "And I'll kill him for it."

I gasp weakly. Not because of the words, or the deadened way he said them.

He means it.

Mother of God, he *really* fucking means it.

This isn't like before, all those years ago. He isn't the same teenager that swore to kill his father for me. No, that boy had fear in his eyes as he'd said it. He tried to hide it, but I remember picking up on it loud and clear.

That boy might have made up his mind to kill, but he hadn't been ready for it.

This man, however . . .

The intercom on his desk goes off again. "Mr. Drevlow. Your 10:30am is here."

He has no assistant yet. Well, he *had* no assistant until today, and apparently the reception at the lobby has been screening all his appointments and calls.

It's been made abundantly clear I won't be doing any of that, therefore reception will be handling that until I hire my assistant.

"Grab your notepad. I want you in here for this one," Andrew says and turns to head back to his desk. "Send her up," he says into the intercom.

I'm still reeling from his promise of murder, but I do as he says and follow him inside.

He leans in front of his desk again. "Lexi, I need you to look me in the eyes."

Taken aback, I do, and I'm struck silent by the plea I see in them. "I need you to trust me and work with me. Please, remember it's all part of the plan."

"What are you—"

Behind me, the elevator opens, and I hear the sound of heels clicking on the floor.

I see something akin to panic flash in Andrew's eyes. "Lexi, just go with me on this one. Show her a united front. And please, *trust me*."

"Drew, I couldn't believe it when you called."

I recognize that voice with every fiber of my being. How could I not? I've come to *loathe* it. Disbelieving, I whirl around.

Kaylee Whittacker slams to a halt at the glass wall, her blue eyes wide and her mouth falling open at the sight of me.

"*You bitch.*"

chapter 57

<u>lexi</u>

present

15 hours before barnard wellington's disappearance

"**a**pologize to her," Andrew warns behind me. "Right. Now."

Is he fucking serious? He's asking *me* to apologize to *her*? Raw, sadistic rage, the likes of which I've never felt, incinerates the blood in my veins. The agony razes through me, obliterating my humanity.

Betrayal. It makes no sense, but I choke on this insane feeling of betrayal.

Blood rushing to my face, I spin around—

He's glaring at Kaylee, not me.

A smidgen of reason breaks through. *I thought it, but . . . I didn't really say that?* No. Apparently, those words came from her.

"Drew, are you serious?" she asks.

I hate the way she's fucking talking to him, all that familiarity, as if they're still close. The fury that had begun to dissipate reignites, a thousand times more powerful than before. Did he stay in contact with her? Remain friends?

Something more?

I'm shaking. About to collapse from the sheer bloodlust flooding me.

Stephen remained friends with her. Works with her. Fucks her.

She actually grew up enough to become the head of her father's company.

But Stephen was never stupid enough to allow her in front of me. I haven't seen the bitch since we were in school together.

Andrew comes to a stop next to me. "Kaylee, I really, really would love for our companies to do business together. But that can't happen if you can't respect Lexi. She's now my right hand and I expect everyone we work with to respect us both." There's no room for negotiation in that tone.

Battling for control, I rip my stare off the floor and focus on Kaylee. She's glaring at me and Andrew. More accurately, at the half-an-inch of space he left between our bodies.

She was always beautiful with her black hair and blue eyes, but for a second, her expression twists, showing a glimpse of the ugliness within.

"We stand to make billions together, Kaylee."

Ugh. He's using that same "logical" tone he used with me earlier.

Inhaling deeply, Kaylee leashes her aggression. I see the moment the jealousy and hatred in her dark blue eyes morphs into greed. Whatever Andrew is offering to let her partner on, it's clearly more attractive to her than our mutual hatred.

She faces me, expression flattening into a composed mask, and she says, "I apologize, Ms. Berkman."

Well. Well. Well. Ms. Kaylee Whittacker has actually become a businesswoman. My surprise at her self-control must show on my face, because her lips twitch with what I can only assume is annoyance.

"Thank you, Kaylee. Now, if we're all ready?" Andrew poses it as a question, but he's already walking toward the sitting area at the other end of his office.

Kaylee follows him willingly, her covetous eyes eating up his tall, large form.

I blink, surprised to find my hand fisting tightly around my notepad.

And, no. It has nothing to do with her presence anymore.

Shit. Am I actually pissed off at the fact that she's sexually molesting him with her eyes?

Yes.

Yes, I am.

I'm as angry about that as I am at the thought that they remained close this whole time.

Kaylee sits on the black sofa, facing the wall.

Andrew stops next to the sofa opposite, waiting for me.

Something loosens in my gut.

Composing myself, I walk there and sit down on the couch. Andrew takes the seat next to me, less than a foot away.

Kaylee's eyes flash momentarily to the space left between his thigh and mine. Other than that, she gives no other outward reaction.

She's going to run to tell Stephen about this. The thought blindsides me out of nowhere, and I can barely maintain my composed facade. Of course she is. God, how could Andrew even think that working with her is a good idea?

My eyes flicker in his direction. Is that what he planned? Why he brought her here?

Andrew leans forward, bracing his arms on his knees. "Your company is one of the best when it comes to platform development."

Kaylee lights up like a fucking Christmas tree at his compliment.

"That's why I want to partner with you on our biggest project yet."

No. Come on. He can't be serious.

"Drew," Kaylee *breathes*, eyes sparkling. "Rumors have been spreading for months about your Providence project. The entire market is on *fire* with speculation as to what you're actually creating."

"Exactly, Kaylee. And I want your company to be a part of that."

Apparently, he *is* serious.

He just asked one of Menahan's biggest allies to join our project. Is he out of his damned mind?

"Jesus, Drew. I can't believe you would trust me with this." She places her hand on her heart, still looking at him like he's her hero.

I've been fisting my pen the entire time, mute. When Andrew smiles at her, I don't give a damn that the smile never reaches his eyes. I still want to jam my pen into one of them.

"That being said, Kaylee. I do have to ask. Will working with me be an issue in regards to your on-going contracts with Menahan?"

chapter 58

lexi

present

1+ hours before barnard wellington's disappearance

t some point during the last hour, I started taking notes on my pad. I have no idea what I'm writing down, but I figure that pretending to be useful is better than the alternative—sitting here, consumed by my anger.

Kaylee's fawning over him, acting like everything he says is the best idea she's ever heard. And the hunger in her eyes . . .

One thing is disgustingly blatant. If I never actually had that dick and I couldn't forget it, imagine how much worse it is on her end. She had it once.

"Drew, is that your bathroom back there?" she asks.

Andrew nods. "By all means."

Another besotted smile and then she's gone.

Andrew turns to face me immediately, his hand landing on my knee. "Lexi."

I jerk away, hissing, "Don't touch me!"

He grabs my waist, holding me in place. "It's all part of the endgame, baby," he whispers for my ears only.

I'm out of my fucking mind, that's the only explanation I have for what leaves my mouth next. "She still wants to fuck you."

His eyes widen, then flash with hunger. He yanks me to him, until there's nothing but an inch between our faces. "You know I don't want her." His breath fans across my lips as he speaks.

I'm irrational, and I'm aware of it. Still doesn't mean I can find enough self-control to shut the hell up. "You're letting her in on the Providence project!"

Andrew's hand slides down my side, past the hem of my skirt. My entire body vibrates as he caresses my thigh.

"A-Andrew? What are you doing?"

His eyes drop to my lips, full of that seething, unsettling intensity. "Lexi, I'm going to kiss you now."

My eyes dart in the direction of his bathroom door.

Still closed.

Instead of rejecting him outright, I ask, "Why?"

His lips quirk but the rest of his expression remains the same— serious. Determined. "I'll finish explaining everything later. For now, I'm going to kiss you. Now, say yes."

Odd, confusing man. He's pretty much telling me he's taking this kiss from me, but he still wants me to agree to it.

His hand tightens around my thigh and his thumb slips under the hem of my dress. "Say yes, baby."

My lips part slowly on a stuttering breath, and my crossed legs press together tightly, locking his thumb between them. With a rotating heart, and a demonic instinct demanding that I push this man back on this couch and mount him, I fight for the strength needed to resist him.

To say no.

When I finally manage to speak, I'm not even surprised to hear what leaves my mouth in a tiny whisper. "*Yes.*"

His brow snaps down, a pain groaned seemingly ripped from him.

And then his lips are on my mine again, tongue slipping straight inside my mouth. I can't hold back my hungry moan, can't stop my nails from sinking into his shoulders and bringing him closer . . .

Hand painfully tight around my thigh, he twines his tongue slowly with mine. Licking me. Teasing me. His harsh breaths mix with my frantic ones, but despite that insane, leashed aggression I feel in him, he keeps this kiss soft.

Passionate but gentle.

My nails sink deeper into his skin with my frustration. Mindless, I shift closer, biting down on his lip hard—

He yanks away from me, pupils blown, chest pumping. Our sides remain close together, no space between us.

Dear God, I almost launch myself at him, that's how painful this is. How unbearable the hole in my being feels. I wanted him all these years, even if I couldn't admit it to myself, but now it's back full force.

An addiction reawakened.

A need grown crazier.

I'm still fucking reeling when the bathroom door opens and Kaylee steps out.

Immediately, her eyes fall to Andrew's still-racing chest. Then, down, down, locking on his crotch.

It takes me two seconds to identify the murderous intent roaring in my veins.

When she can pull her eyes away from his swollen, needy cock, she takes in how our bodies are touching. How Andrew is still angled toward me.

Eyes flashing, she stares at my lips.

At my no doubt swollen, *wet* lips.

Andrew makes no move to put space between us.

And as Kaylee makes her way back to the couch, her hands fisted at her sides, I realize:

He did this on purpose, too.

Don't know how I know, but Kaylee was probably talking to Menahan in that bathroom. I wouldn't be surprised if it actually turns out that she's spying on us for him.

Something Andrew also suspects and he wanted her to see this.

He wanted her to know.

She's going to run to inform Stephen that we're intimate—and Andrew-fucking-Drevlow was betting on it.

chapter 59

<u>andrew</u>
7 years ago

My father's back slams onto the porch.

I land on top of him. Before I even make contact, I'm already wailing on him. My fist collides with his mouth and I swear I hear the impact echo.

A lifetime of rage. Of hate. At least fourteen years building up to this point.

And my father laughs.

His lips split in a wide smile, even as blood floods his mouth and coats his teeth. "You'll never find her."

He tries to block my next hit.

He fails.

I get three more hits in before Finn and my father's bodyguards make it to the porch. The bodyguards grab me. They manage to jerk me off him.

Growling, I throw my weight back, taking one of the guards with me across the porch. His body rams into the railing. The weight of me slamming into his midsection knocks the wind out of him.

The other two come at me.

"No! Stop!" My father gets to his feet, wiping a hand across his bloody mouth. "The boy thinks that he's finally a man. Let him up."

Foolish, egotistical bastard. I've been training my body to destroy him for years now.

Even if I didn't know it.

I feel my lips twist into a bitter smirk. "Do yourself a favor and tell me where she is."

My father sneers. "Never."

I've never moved so fast in my life.

Hands fisting his blazer, I send us both flying down the stairs and onto the cement walkway leading to the porch. My arm scrapes across concrete.

I barely feel it.

My father wraps his hands around my neck to immobilize me.

Too late.

I slam my foot into his stomach, sending him flying sideways onto the grass. Just as fast, I'm on top of him again, my fist connecting with his head. "TELL ME WHERE SHE IS!"

His fist collides with my face but that's the only hit he gets in before self-preservation takes over. Trying to shield his head with his arms, he screams back, "Never! Even if I did know, I'd never tell you!"

I pause.

He doesn't know where she is. He might have helped her get away from here as fast as possible, but he doesn't know her final destination.

My hands latch around his neck and I begin squeezing down with all my strength. "You. Will. Find. Her."

Face red, veins bulging, my father claws at my arms.

"You're going to put every single asset you command to use. You're going to locate her and you're going to do it RIGHT THE FUCK NOW!"

Somehow, as he's suffocating, skin turning purple, he manages to shake his head.

No.

A single world and suddenly my father's life loses its value.

An entire lifetime of pain whispers to me. Tells me that this is worth it. That he deserves this.

Finn screams out behind me, "You'll never find her if you go to jail for killing him!"

The words register. I know he's being logical. That he has a point.

My hands tighten around my father's neck, almost as if separated from my body. As if I was *born* to end this man's life and now that destiny has come knocking, there is no denying my life's purpose.

Disjointed thoughts echo in my head. *Need to kill him. End him. Make him suffer. Make him pay.*

Hands grab my shoulders and I feel a sting in my neck. Immediately, there's a rush beneath my skin, a cold sensation.

I jerk back, raising one hand to elbow whoever is behind me.

The world's spinning but it doesn't matter. I'm back to choking my father, ignoring his attempts to buck me off.

Harder. Harder. He's struggling now. Losing consciousness . . .

More hands grab me.

Another prick to the other side of my neck.

Enraged, I realize what they're doing to me.

I'm being drugged. Tranquilized so I won't kill that bastard for what he's done.

I roar, trying to break loose—

Something slams into my stomach, knocking the air and the last of my fight out of me.

Body falling limp, I struggle to stay awake, even as a black van pulls up at the curve and I'm dragged toward it.

My father's hoarse voice reaches me through the fog. "Get him back to the fucking house where I can set him straight."

"Mr. Drevlow," Finn interrupts.

My father isn't hearing it. "I'm sorry Mr. Walsh, this has nothing to do with you. This is family business."

"But where are you—"

"Have a good day, Mr. Walsh."

I'm lifted and thrown into the back of the van, face up. Struggling to stay awake, I lift my head—

Just in time to see Finn's worried expression right before the door is slid closed.

I last exactly three more seconds after that.

The last thought going through my head is Lexi's name.

chapter 60

lexi

present

5 hours before barnard wellington's disappearance

What a fucking crazy day.

Exhausted, I walk into my loft, dropping my keys onto the side table by the door. It's 7:12pm and I'm just getting home.

After the meeting with Kaylee, Andrew spent all day in the medical and pharmaceutical division of the company. He was overseeing my mother's transfer. At around 2:00pm, as I was in the middle of looking through my new assistant's resume, he called me downstairs.

My mother is now on the thirty-sixth floor of Drevlow Systems, Inc. Six floors beneath my new office. When I walked into the room they're keeping her in, and I saw the tube inserted into her side, my legs gave out.

Most fucked up part? Andrew was there to catch me.

Tears spring to my eyes. "Don't think about it," I tell myself, walking tiredly toward my living room. My massive desktop is in one corner, on the desk in front of the exposed brick wall.

My heart thunders as I get closer because I know what I'm about to do.

I know what it's going to cost me.

But it's about damn time I find out the truth of what exactly happened all those years ago.

For the first time ever, doubt creeps in. *What if he's innocent? What if . . . you ran away from him and it all wasn't really his fault?*

Then everything that happened to me the last seven years would be all *my* fault.

Tears start leaking down my cheeks, hot trails of misery and fear, but it doesn't stop me. I didn't have a chance to talk to Andrew after Kaylee left. I have no idea what his plan is.

What I do know is that that man looks at me like I'm the only reason he's still here.

What I do know is that six years ago, something really fucked up happened to him and it changed the boy I once loved.

I also know I *watched* the video of Andrew confessing to the cops.

But something isn't adding up. The neat little version of events I convinced myself were the facts are systematically falling apart.

Dropping into my chair, I fire up my computer. As soon as it's online, I open my browser and start typing.

His name and our senior year. The year I disappeared.

I figure if I start there and work my way forward, the pieces of the puzzle will begin falling into place.

Immediately, on top of the results, there's a slew of YouTube videos.

Sitting closer to the monitor, I squint, disbelieving of what I'm seeing . . .

One specific video seems to show Andrew on top of . . . on top of his father?

The title of the video proves my suspicion of what that thumbnail is showing me.

Mr. Drevlow and his heir caught on video fighting.

Jesus. Seriously?

Wait a second . . . I click open the link to the YouTube page for that video.

"Oh. My. Fucking. God." I struggle to breath as I take in where this fight took place.

The yard of my old home.

Shaking, I click play.

Whoever took the video must have missed the beginning of the fight. Andrew is on top of his father, landing punch after punch. Suddenly, he roars in a demon's voice, "TELL ME WHERE SHE IS!"

I choke on a sob.

One of the bodyguards comes up to the person recording and demands they stop, but not before I hear, "You. Will. Find. Her. You're going to put every single asset you command to use. You're going to locate her and you're going to do it RIGHT THE FUCK NOW!"

The video ends, no doubt because the person recording was forced to shut it off.

Shaking, freezing deep in my soul, I return to Google to continue my search.

I know who Andrew is talking about. I know that he was demanding his father find me.

Insane. Mad with loss.

I barely saw his eyes on that video but there was no denying it.

He was shattered by my disappearance.

My shaking fingers are clumsy as I pull up headline after

headline. Article after article. The accident six years ago was national news. I remember where I was that year. It was the first year that I started working for Stephen and his now-deceased father.

Willingly.

He hadn't raped me yet. Hadn't infected my mother. Hadn't forced me to go into a binding contract to try and keep me under his thumb.

As I was finishing my first year at college, Stephen convinced me he was innocent in the whole thing.

That Kaylee and Andrew planned it all along.

Barnard backed up his story.

And I, stupid, lonely, naive bitch that I was, allowed Stephen to convince me that working for his father's company would keep me safe.

Would keep me hidden.

Only one of those two promises turned out to be true.

That same year, Andrew Drevlow nearly died.

By the time I drag myself to bed, the room spinning, it's 12:22am. As I collapse onto my bed, still clothed, face drenched in tears, I've finally admitted to myself the truth.

Six years ago, Andrew Drevlow slammed his Porsche into a concrete divider at ninety-seven miles per hour.

And I think it was because of me.

chapter 61

<u>lexi</u>

present

1 hour after barnard wellington's death

a pinprick on my thigh. Cold liquid beneath my skin.

Swallowing, I try to open my eyes. My lids are heavy. So heavy. I focus on my window, the one facing the fire escape. On the moonlight pouring in.

It's . . . it's open?

Another prick in my arm.

Whimpering, I roll over.

"I'm so sorry baby. I have no choice."

I squint at the large figure sitting next to me on my bed. "A-Andrew?" Why can't I focus? Why is everything so blurry?

"Shhhh." He leans over me, caressing my cheek. "It's over," he mumbles, talking more to himself than to me. "Had to. Have to make sure he can't take you now that I've hurt him."

What?

Andrew begins easing away.

"No!" My voice comes out slurred. I try sitting up but everything is too heavy. I'm too weak. Frantic to keep him with me, I grab his wrist. "Was d-dreaming about . . . you."

Andrew exhales and returns to me, the light from the moon illuminating his face.

His . . . his eyes. They're even darker than before, despite the fact that they're glowing almost gold in the moonlight. Something's off in his stare. Crazier. "What were you dreaming about, baby?"

My breath hisses and my back arches. I'm so tired. So sleepy. Yet I can't fight this hunger. "You were taking . . . me. Showing me pleasure again."

A choked groan echoes in my room. "Fuck, Lexi. You're out of it. Can't—"

I fist the sleeve of his white button down. Is . . . is that dirt on his sleeve? Can't tell. Pulling on his shirt, I rub my thighs together, trying to ease the ache. "Only you."

Shuddering, he leans closer, his eyes screaming that he loves me. That he needs me. That he can't live without me anymore than I can live without him. "Only me what, baby?"

Fighting for strength, I raise my hand, my arm feeling like it weighs a hundred pounds. It's always so hard moving in my dreams. I'm always too weak. Defenseless.

My heart breaks with that realization.

I'm dreaming. He isn't really here.

Doesn't matter. I *need* to touch him.

When my hand makes contact with his face, we both exhale with relief. "No one's ever felt good. Only you."

Andrew tenses. "Because it's only been me and Stephen, and that bastard abused you."

I pull on his shirt again, whimpering pathetically when he refuses to come closer. Shaking my head, I slip one hand down, out of control, needing to touch my pussy.

Andrew's eyes land on where my hand is slipping under my skirt, that madness in his stare spreading.

"I-I tried." Moaning, I play with my clit over my panties.

"What the fuck do you mean you tried?"

The anger in his tone makes me hornier. More desperate. "Tried to feel with someone else, but felt nothing. It's you, Drew. It's only ever been you."

A constant, almost-purring sound reaches my ears as he finally, *finally*, leans down. He cups my neck gently, but the way he's holding me frightens me.

Still groaning, he kisses my lips, and my fear disappears instantly. "Who?" He growls, rubbing our lips together. Is that cigarette smoke I taste on his breath? "Who did you try with?"

It's just a dream, but somehow I know I can't answer that. My instinct tells me I'll be putting Paul's life in danger if I do. "Please. Please. Make me come again, Drew. I *need* it."

He shakes his head, hand tightening around my neck. "You can't do this, Andrew. She's out of it from the shot. Don't take advantage."

His words are low, mumbled. Confusing.

I don't care. Growling, I force his hand between my legs.

A broken moan escapes him.

I cry out, coming instantly.

"*Fucccck*, Lexi. Fuck!" He flies away from me, leaving me frantically undulating on the bed.

Yanking my thighs apart, he falls between them. My thong is tugged to the side.

And then it's his tongue on me again, piercing me with unbelievable pleasure. My hands fall to cup the back of his head, holding him against me. "*Drew. Drew. Drew.*" I thrust my hips against his face, rubbing all over his tongue. "Eat it, baby. Eat my pussy, Drew."

He growls out against me, making out with my cunt, his moans just as out of control as my own.

"Oh God. Oh God. Drew. Coming again!"

An animal's snarl vibrates along my pulsating cunt.

I cry his name one more time, my heart stuttering in my chest . . .

It all recedes just as quick as it hits, leaving me boneless. Weak. Heaviness presses in on all sides.

Drew moves away and the sudden cold I feel at his absence makes me want to cry.

So long without you . . . Can't take it anymore . . .

The last thing I remember is the sound of my voice, begging him to please stay.

chapter 62

lexi
present

i stare at the girl in the bathroom mirror and cringe.

No bones about it. I look like utter shit.

But that's what a night of back-to-back wet dreams does to a girl.

"Stupid, Lexi. So stupid." I practically drag myself out of the bathroom. Like a mindless zombie, I head toward my kitchen, mind fixated on coffee.

And those two dreams from last night.

Fuck. The second one felt so real.

No surprise, I woke up with a soaked pussy. I think I actually came in my sleep.

From a creepy, twisted wet dream featuring Andrew Drevlow *injecting* me with something before eating my pussy out until I saw stars.

That's it. Introspection is bad. I pause by the living room and turn on the TV, leaving it on the news. Need something to drown out the thoughts and distract me.

Popping the little K-Cup into the machine, I choose the ten-ounce option and fire the machine up.

The heavenly smell almost cheers me up.

Almost.

Usually, just the smell of coffee is enough to set my world to rights. For a little while, at least.

Regardless of the fact that I took a cold shower, my body still aches. My pussy is tender, almost as if it *was* kissed and sucked last night.

Or it could just be years of neglect. I never gave myself willingly to Stephen. Never. Even after he broke me, all he ever had was the dead sex doll he loved to fuck. The one that stared at him blankly and gave no reaction except for when he turned brutal.

Eventually, he accepted it. Hated me for it, made it very clear, but he took the little I had to give.

It was never about *my* pleasure with him. Could never be. And not just because he forced himself on me, abused me.

He just wasn't capable of making me feel anything good, and he hated both Andrew and I more because of that.

Scowling at the reminder of how little pleasure I've had in my life, I pull my mug out of the machine.

"Yes. And this just coming in. New Jersey's own Barnard Wellington, CFO of Menahan Industries, has been reported missing."

I gasp sharply, fingers going numb.

The mug slips out of my hand. Almost in slow motion, I watch it fly toward the ground, coffee arching out of it.

The glass shatters on impact.

The hot liquid drenches my foot; scalding me, I'm sure. But I don't feel anything other than that cold shock.

TWISTED HEARTBREAK

"Reports claim that the elusive CFO of Menahan Industries had been in hiding for months now."

Because he refused to pay an old debt. 'Til this day, I haven't been able to find out *who* he owes money to. All I know is that about six months ago, Barnard stopped coming into work entirely. We were all told he'd be working remotely from home.

Then, two days later, I overheard Stephen arguing on the phone with Barnard about his debt.

"Sources also claim that Mr. Wellington has only been missing for about five hours. At this time, there are no leads or suspects. Authorities request that anyone with information please contact—"

I stop paying attention. Ignoring my red, wet foot and the mess on my floor, I run back to my room to find my phone. It's still on the charger. Ripping it off the nightstand, I find three texts from Paul.

Paul: Have you seen the news?

Paul: Apparently Stephen is pushing authorities to treat this as a missing person's case although it's only been a few hours.

There goes that sentence again. A few hours. My eyes take in the time—7:26am. A few hours ago, I think I was deep in that second dream . . . What if it wasn't a dream?

Don't be stupid, Lexi, I tell myself. There were no signs of someone being here when I awoke. Nothing but a phantom pain on the inside of my arm where that needle pricked me in my dream.

I already checked three times; there's no marks on the inside of my arm. Needles always leave marks. *Don't they?* Heart pounding, I read Paul's third text.

Paul: Lexi, did you by any chance tell our new boss about what Menahan did to you?

No, I didn't, but he guessed it all on his own.

Oh my God. Does Andrew have something to do with this? I think back on the video, how he fought his own father for me . . and my gut shouts out, *Of course he has something to do with it!*

I'm not due into work until 8:30am.

Fuck it.

Rushing into my closet, I throw on the first thing I can find and run into the bathroom to fix my hair.

chapter 63

<u>andrew</u>
present

i watch the news on one of my many monitors as New Jersey society implodes into chaos, and I can't help the smirk that tugs on my lips.

That fucking asshole honestly thinks he can flush me out by making this a public scandal. What he doesn't realize is that I already knew he would do this. Expected and *planned* for it.

The body hasn't been found. I don't know if it ever will be. Suppose it's up to the mafia and how much of an example they want to make out of him.

But I know Stephen is aware of his death. Considering he now also knows I found out what he did to my Lexi, I'm sure he put two-and-two together and came up with the right answer: *Andrew Drevlow killed your best friend, asshole.*

One of many. Not only do I plan to kill everyone that hurt Lexi—I plan to take down anyone that even thinks of getting in the way of that.

My plan puts Lexi in danger. Stephen is going to want her back twice as bad now. That's why I had no choice.

I shift in my seat and rub my head, trying to ignore the taste of delicious pussy still lingering in my mouth.

Fuck, man. It's bad enough that I snuck in there five hours ago and drugged her with the same shit my father once used on me the day we fought . . . but did I have to practically molest her while at it?

Shit, but she went *wild* at my presence. I'd just injected the nano-tracker into her arm when those big-grays shot open and stared at me like I'm her everything.

Then she started begging.

Confessing.

My jaw clenches as I remember everything she said. Who was the other asshole she tried to be with? God help me, was it more than one man?

How many soon-to-be-dead guinea pigs did she experiment with before she realized none of them could ever work out for her? Because none of them were *me.*

That new, demented, blood-thirsty voice echoes in my head. *Kill them. All of them.* Fucking hypocritical since only God knows how many women I fucked in her absence, trying to just deal with the catastrophic hole she left in my heart and brain.

But . . . "Fuck!" I need a goddamn cigarette. Face burning with rage, I send my mug flying into the wall. My broken mind spins on its axles.

Guilt. Love. Desperation. Fury. More guilt.

I smother my face with my hands and groan. Originally, I'd resolved not to stalk her beyond the tracker in her car, but then I realized that Stephen might find a way to get to her.

To take her.

And Asad? I have an entire file with information on that sadistic, perverted bastard. After the way he stared at my girl, I can't rest easy. If it wasn't for the fact that his company is secretly under contract to develop nano-tech for Menahan, I wouldn't be dealing with him at all.

I struggled with my decision to inject her with the tracker, but at the end of the day, it was necessary.

Damn me to hell, *molesting* her in her drugged-up state wasn't! I don't even know the details of what Stephen did to her, but that stark despair in her eyes tells me that it was extensive. Brutal.

And here I fucking come, manhandling her in the back of her truck, practically mouth-raping her with my cock, then taking advantage of her last night.

She begged me to stay. My already cracked heart breaks a little more at that thought. *Don't lose it. Keep it together for her. Ensure her safety.* Heart pumping with violent pain, I pull up the tracking software on my phone.

Just as I recognize what I'm seeing, the elevator doors open.

Most people would tell you that the sound of heels clicking is all the same. Doubt that's true 'cause every time I hear her walking, my body recognizes it's her immediately.

She came early.

Lexi comes into view, looking as exhausted as I feel. Stopping at the glass wall, she ignores it as it automatically slides open. Instead, she focuses on the mess of ceramic and coffee on the floor by the wall.

Her eyebrow rises.

No time. I need her ready by tonight. So, without giving her a chance to even speak, I rise from my seat. "Good morning. Get your tablet ready. We need to start planning."

That raised eyebrow turns in my direction. "Planning?"

"Yes."

chapter 64

lexi

present

h e made me come all over his tongue in that dream.

It's all I can think about as he paces in front of me, his tall, muscular body encased in that charcoal suit.

He's talking about some event he's going to tonight on behalf of the company; that much I know. His raspy, deep voice has become the perfect backdrop to my pounding heart.

My phone's vibrating in my palm. I'm busy pretending I'm taking notes as Drew speaks.

In reality, I'm watching the headlines come in, one after the other, thanks to the alert I set on my phone.

I dare a quick peek at my notifications bar.

Barnard Wellington Missing.

Son of Corporate Tycoon Had Been in Hiding Prior to Disappearing.

Barnard Wellington: Everything You Need to Know About His Fall.

My heart races harder and I quickly return my attention to Drew, my mind a confused whirlwind of contradicting thoughts.

I don't know why, but I know this has to do with you. Bullshit. I know why. The psychosis in his eyes when I refused to tell him what Stephen did to me is one I'll never forget.

God damn it. Your tongue. I had forgotten how good it feels. He made me feel pleasure for the first time in seven years.

First, in the back of my car.

Then, he began haunting my dreams again.

Fuck. That dream seemed so *real.* As if he'd actually been in my room, eating my pussy so lovingly.

You're my enemy. Yet he decided to help my mother of his own volition, before I even asked him to. The gratitude is still a heady sensation in my veins. I want him, this man who is my enemy. This man that once betrayed me.

I shouldn't. God help me, I shouldn't. Hating him is second nature. Has been for the last seven years. It hasn't gone away.

I think I hate him even more now because all I can think about is walking up to him and biting that sexy, thick neck.

I'd do it hard. Mark him. Possibly draw blood.

"I'll need you to come with me to the event tonight."

His words slap me out of my sex-starved haze. "No." Like hell I'll be caught alone with him outside of work.

Drew slows in his pacing. Then, he comes to a full stop, his head swiveling in my direction. "*Excuse me?*" His eyes are hard. His jaw clenches. This is my *boss* glaring in outrage at my denial.

My entire body tenses on the chair, preparing for battle, every instinct aware of his aggression rising in the room. "I read your calendar and the briefs of what that event is going to entail. You don't need me with you."

But *I* need distance. Time to myself. Looking at him is enough to erase any sexual trauma. I feared sex for so long.

Yet now I'm crazed to suck his cock.

Writhe on it.

"You're right. I don't *need* you with me for this event." He starts walking to me and something about his gait seems cruel. "What I do need is you by my side." Drew grabs the armrests and leans down, trapping me with that ruthless, unrelenting gaze. "At all times. I went seven years without you—don't ask me to spend another needless minute more."

"What?" I snap, annoyed at his closeness. At the things he makes me want to do. "You're planning on moving in, too, just to keep me close?"

His lips twitch and all I want to do is rub my clit on them. "Don't tempt me, baby."

My thighs quiver. I tense them, knowing that he'll see if I press them together. My pussy aches so bad my teeth start grinding. "I have a choice." The statement holds no authority, just the softness of a woman in heat.

God damn, his fucking scent.

I press back into the chair, desperate for some space.

Drew's eyes search mine, before falling to my lips. I gasp as he bites his bottom lip slowly.

He's going to kiss me.

If he does, I'm going to snap and attack him. Force him to fuck me right on his desk.

He's still staring at my lips, his pupils slowly expanding.

Panicking, I blurt out the first thing that comes to mind. "If you want me to go to the event, you'll answer a question for me and you'll answer it honestly."

He backs up a bit at that, seeming surprised. "I'm your boss, remember?" His eyebrow quirks with amusement.

I glare at him and push against his chest until he finally eases away from me. "You want me here more than I want to be here."

His eyes flash with pain and I blink in surprise at the regret I feel. "You're probably right about that, baby."

That fucking word. The way he says it.

As if seven years didn't pass. As if he never betrayed me. As if we're still back there, in the field, where he's making all his pretty, glittery promises and pretending I'm his world.

But God. What if he didn't betray me?

You are *his world.* No idea where that thought came from but I shove it down. "If you want me to come, tell me. Where's Barnard Wellington right now?"

chapter 65

lexi

present

a ndrew distances himself, but not before I see his pupils shrinking with dread. "What do you mean?" His tone is casual.

I don't know why, but his attempt at lying to me is like a kick to the chest. Suddenly furious, I stand and deposit my notepad and phone onto my seat. "Don't play stupid. The whole world knows he's missing by now."

And fuck. Even *Paul*, a person that doesn't know my history with Andrew, suspects he had something to do with it. Something Paul saw in Andrew must have given him the vibe that he would be capable of this.

Andrew opens his mouth to speak; I hold up a hand, stopping him. "And let me tell you something right now. If you even try to lie to me again, you'll be putting me in a position of never, ever trusting you."

His chest rises and falls with a sigh. "You already don't trust me."

Maybe it's the dream still fucking with my head. Maybe it's this insane craving I have to bounce on his dick—*literally.*

Hell, maybe it's because I'm sick and tired of feeling so alone in this world, but once again I blurt out the truth. "I want to."

His expression softens. "*Lexi.*"

The intercom beeps. "The delivery you're expecting is here, Mr. Drevlow. As well as Ms. Rhines." My new assistant.

Shit. It's 9:00am already? The last half-hour went by insanely fast.

"Thank you. Send the delivery up first. Then send Ms. Rhines up in five minutes." He walks back in my direction. Stopping a foot away from me, he crosses his arms, biceps bulging with strain beneath the dark gray fabric of his blazer.

I can't help but get the feeling that he's holding himself back from touching me.

"You're right, Lexi. I'm sorry."

Don't know what I expected but, oh my fucking God. Was that a confirmation?

The elevator opens and within seconds, a huge Spanish man in a black suit appears. He's carrying a big, white box in one hand. In the other, he's holding two shopping bags—a cardboard one with the Christian Louboutin logo on it and a smaller aqua bag that would be unmistakable anywhere.

Andrew motions for the packages to be left on my desk.

My mouth falls open.

Grabbing my chin gently, he turns my head back in his direction. "I'll be working with Ms. Rhines to get her up to speed on my calendar and such. That"—he nods at the items on my desk—"is your outfit for tonight. You'll need to leave two hours early to start getting ready."

When he turns to walk back to his desk, I have to literally shake my head to refocus. "Andrew!"

He stops right next to his desk.

"Are you confirming you have something to do with it?" I ask, my voice shaking.

He continues walking around to his chair. Once before it, he stops and aims those toffee-colored eyes my way. "Yes, Lexi. I am."

I swear to God the ground tilts. "W-why? To bring down Menahan?" He's willing to go *this* far? Risk this much? This is no longer just a private war between two frighteningly powerful CEOs. This . . . this has become utterly public.

"Yes. To bring him down. And"—he sits on his throne and smooths a hand down his lapel, as calm as can be—"because he helped hurt you, Lexi." His eyes seem to shimmer in the bright daylight pouring in from the floor-to-ceiling windows. "They're all going to pay."

All speech deserts me as my reality once again realigns itself.

"Ms. Rhines will be here shortly. I promise we'll talk more about this later."

Normally, I wouldn't drop it. I'd push and push until he gave me all the information.

Normally.

Right now I'm pretty sure I'm fucking shattered and I'm not allowing myself to process it.

In a daze, I grab my things and walk toward the sliding glass door.

"Oh, and Lexi?"

I pause right at the door.

"That right there is Mateo. He's your new bodyguard."

Because now I need one?

Of course I do.

Another elevator opens and a young brunette walks inside.

"Get used to his presence, Lexi. He'll be with you everywhere you go from now on."

Still reeling, I avoid my new assistant's stare, walk back to my desk, and plop down on my chair.

Mateo, expression stoic, walks to the sitting area in front of my desk and calmly sits on the couch. Making himself comfortable, he pulls out his phone and gets busy doing . . . whatever the hell it is resting bodyguards do.

"Ms. Rhines, please come in," Andrew says from within his office, and I realize she was standing there, looking at me have a stoic mental breakdown.

My eyes bounce off the packages on my desk, my heart racing so hard my chest hurts with each hit.

I'm way over my head. Lord help me, it's time I admit that no part of this is under my control.

None.

I really did escape the hold of one tyrant, only to end up in the clutches of another.

chapter 66

lexi
present

i'm supposed to be on my way out. Need to get home and get dressed. Prepare myself for this event, a meeting of powerful people all donating to the Holtzman Charity. In reality, it's the scene of whatever plot Andrew is hatching, and the guest list confirmed it.

Menahan will be there.

So will Kaylee.

I'm not ready to face Stephen, but Andrew isn't giving me the choice. Logically, I understand that whatever he's planning, he needs me there. But it isn't just about the plan. Andrew wants to hurt Stephen and me being there is the kind of blow that will keep Stephen off balance.

Luckily for Andrew, I want to hurt Stephen just as bad.

However, that doesn't make dealing with how fast things are moving any easier.

"I'm telling you, Lexi." Mom pauses, struggling to catch her breath.

I fight to keep my eyes on her face. That oxygen mask is nowhere near as jarring as seeing the tube inserted into her.

"He cares about you. He's going to help you."

It's funny how years ago, my mother lost trust in Andrew. Had come to believe that he was no different than his father. But over the last three years, something began changing her mind. Little by little, she became "Team Andrew" and I never understood why.

Now I suspect.

Grabbing her hand, I struggle to maintain my calm. Upsetting her isn't an option right now. They started her on an even more aggressive ART regimen this morning. I can only guess the sheer amount of antivirals they're pumping her with. "Mom . . . I need to ask you something and I need you to be one-hundred-percent honest."

Her eyes, the same color as my own, focus directly on me.

"Did you . . . did you know what happened to Andrew six years ago?"

She doesn't answer but the tears that flood her eyes tell me enough.

Shocked, I let go of her hand. I don't know how my heart still has the ability to feel pain, after all the beatings it's taken during my life, but I have to resist the urge to hold a hand to my chest. "Why . . . why didn't you—"

"Tell you?" My mother's voice is a strained whisper. "You didn't want to hear it. A mere mention of his name would send you deeper into that despair. Not even Stephen's abuse could hurt you as bad."

I'm startled to feel two fat tears leak down my cheeks. Now, more than ever, I'm hyperaware of Mateo's huge, silent presence standing by the door. I should be more careful, shouldn't speak with Mom about this while he's here. What if he goes back and tells Drew? Doesn't matter. My emotions decide for me. "Wh-what are you saying?"

"The truth." Mom reaches out for my hand. Seeing how thin and frail it is—how her weak fingers stretch while seeking my own—I can't refuse her. Regardless of how fucked up I am. "And Lexi? He's not like his father." A tear slides down Mom's cheek. "Maybe some parts of him are, but you *matter* to him. Just tell him everything. He'll fix it for you. I *know* he will."

I'm sobbing now. All-out ugly crying. There are no words, just me shaking my head. I can't find the words to tell my mom that Andrew already knows the gist of it. That he's making moves to fix it.

That I suspect his version of "fixing" what happened to me includes murder.

"Lexi." The way Mom squeezes my hand shocks me. The move displays more strength than I thought her capable of. "Whatever he's planning, be by his side. I spoke to him. I saw the look in his eyes. *Trust him.*"

I don't know what to say.

A minute or two passes and then Mateo steps closer to us, clearing his throat. "Ms. Berkman, we need to head out. Mr. Drevlow gave us strict instructions as to what time to be ready."

I didn't even get to talk to him today. Again. He spent the whole morning walking Ms. Rhines through the basics; an event that I hate to admit drove me crazy. Apparently, Andrew Drevlow is obsessed with personally training the people that work closest to him.

Then he headed out an hour ago on an important "errand".

Standing, I lean over and kiss Mom's forehead. "Don't worry, Mom. I plan on doing whatever is necessary to bring down Stephen." I straighten and wipe the tears off my cheeks, shoving my feelings where I always do—deep, deep into the recesses of my mind. "But trusting him isn't a possibility right now. First, I need to find out what's really going on."

Which means getting it through that man's head.

Whatever it is, I can handle it. I've been through much, much worse.

chapter 67

lexi
present

i can't handle this.

What the hell was I thinking earlier?

My ankle twists mid-step. My bodyguard momentarily places his hand on my arm to steady me. I barely notice it. Can't rip my eyes away.

It's just a suit. Nothing more. Stop overreact—Jesus. Look at him.

No, I'm serious. Look. At. Him.

Like the deadly predator he is, Andrew Drevlow steps away from his car, his eyes glowing golden in the street lights.

I can't walk.

Can't breathe.

How did I think I could do this?

"Mr. Drevlow," Mateo says, surprise evident in his tone. He

hadn't expected Andrew here either. It hadn't been the plan. We were supposed to meet Andrew at the Holtzman Manor, where the event is taking place.

Instead, here he is, frozen twenty-feet from me, body wrapped deliciously in that black suit. White button down open and perfect bow-tie. I've seen many men in tuxedos, but there's no denying that Andrew looks like pure sex in them.

His hair is as short as usual, shaved close to his head, but there's stubble covering his jaw.

I haven't moved. He hasn't either. Mateo has gone silent behind me.

Andrew's eyes drop to my feet, where one of my silver, Louboutin peep-toe heels is bared thanks to the slit in my dress. His eyes fixate on that slit, rising very, very slow, up the length of me.

I started shaking as soon as I saw the outfit—from the instinctual knowledge that he picked this out for me. The dress is made of luxurious, soft blue fabric. Not just any blue either.

Royal blue.

The same color as the dress I wore the night of my eighteenth-birthday.

Around my wrists and dangling from my ears is a small fortune in diamonds. My neck was left bare and I can understand why he chose it that way.

The multitude of diamonds sewn into the hem of my bodice are decoration enough.

"Mateo," Andrew snaps, wild eyes locked on my chest. "You'll be following in your car. I'm escorting Ms. Berkman."

"Yes, Sir." Apparently, Mateo knows better than to question the man in front of us.

Even after Mateo walks toward his own car—a huge, black beast that rivals my truck—I can't bring myself to move a muscle. This attraction has blown up inside me again, worse than ever.

TWISTED HEARTBREAK

Lord help Andrew Drevlow, but if I get within a foot of him, I'm going to *maul* him.

Clenching his jaw, he starts walking toward me, each step controlled but determined. It's like watching destiny coming at you full force—you're scared as fuck, utterly unprepared, and yet you lack the strength to run away.

He stops in front of me, chest racing, eyes bouncing all over me like he doesn't know where to focus. Slowly, he raises a hand and runs his fingers down the ends of my hair. I styled it over my shoulder, leaving a hint of curl at the end.

"I miss your curls," he rasps, finally meeting my eyes.

There's no answer to that. I'm busy staring at him, trying to make sense of this. How the fuck can one man have so much power over anyone?

He grabs my hand, groaning low in his chest at the feel of my skin.

That's okay, I guess. It's not like I was able to hold back my breathless whimper, either.

Lexi, you're so fucked, girl. So fucked. Because I'm going to end up fucking this man. There's no doubt. I shouldn't. Really, really shouldn't. Yet who on Earth would be able to control themselves?

"Come." He begins leading me toward his car, that insanely expensive piece of machinery. It's even more expensive-looking than his car all those years ago.

Something I don't need to be thinking about right now. At all.

He opens the door for me. I'm unsteady on my heels as I lower myself into the seat. Once he's come around to his side and settled into the driver's seat, he stares at me silently for a few minutes.

Licking suddenly dry lips, I rasp out the first question that comes to mind, "Why did you change the plan and come to pick me up?" *Why did you catch me off guard in a less crowded setting, blindsiding me?* Maybe if we'd been around more people I would've been distracted.

The car purrs to life. "I couldn't stop myself."

Don't look at him. Don't. You'll lose it. It can't be normal that a person that's been abused as much as I was can feel like this—two breaths away from going rabid and devouring that man.

"I also need to get you up to speed."

That finally makes me look at him. "Oh? You're finally ready to be fully honest?"

His eyes flicker in my direction. "Of course, Lexi. I promised."

"Why?"

"Because, baby, I *need* you to trust me."

chapter 68

lexi
present

the Holtzman Manor is over an hour away from Jersey City. I don't know how much time has passed. All I know is my mind is nearly catatonic from everything I've heard.

I expected that Andrew's plan involved ruinous strikes at Menahan Industries. I'd already begun mapping out a series of cyberattacks designed to possibly infiltrate his systems. Or at the very least, check if the vulnerabilities I knew existed before are still there.

But Andrew isn't just focused on destroying their companies. He wants to destroy all of *them*. He plans to play on the one weakness they obviously still have.

Stephen is obsessed with me.

I thought Andrew planned to lord me over Stephen, yes, but not like this. I'd expected Andrew to play on Stephen's need to control me. Throw it in Stephen's face that I'm working for him now.

But this? It goes deeper.

And Kaylee is obsessed with Andrew. That's ridiculously obvious. She made no move to hide that she was fantasizing about getting him naked.

My hands fist tightly in my lap.

Stephen and Kaylee may screw each other from time-to-time, but it barely means anything. They don't want each other—they want us.

Andrew plans to fuck with their minds by using their emotions against them.

"You . . ." I stare out the window. "You don't just want them to know I'm your right hand. You want them to believe . . . we're together?"

"Yes, Lexi." No hesitation in his answer. No regret.

"You plan on seducing me in front of them to make it seem more real?"

Silence.

Another confirmation.

God, why does that *burn* so badly? "So that's what you've been priming me up for? To put on an act?"

"You think that . . . fucking hell." Out of nowhere, the car swerves off the lane and onto the side of the road. It's a residential neighborhood, but a line of trees blocks my side from view.

"Andrew?"

His seat belt snaps off.

My head flies around and I gasp. Drew is leaning over me, mere inches from my face. His hand lands on my thigh—my bare thigh.

His other hand slides behind my head to fist my hair. "Lexi." Expression strained, he squeezes his eyes shut. "I'm going to kiss you again. Say yes, baby."

Trembling, I whisper, "And what would you do if I said *no*?"

His troubled eyes open. "I'd beg you for forgiveness after."

TWISTED HEARTBREAK

"Are you telling me that you're going to take it anyway, even if I refuse?"

That wet, sexy tongue peeks out to wet his lips. "Yeah." His voice is so deep. So rough. "Fuck me, but yeah, I am." His shallow breaths caress my lips.

My own breaths race. Looking up into his eyes, I raise my hand to his shoulders.

He slides his hand up my thigh, closer to my aching pussy.

Shaking from head-to-toe, I ease my legs apart.

His nostrils flare and the hand wrapped around my hair tightens. The hand on my thigh flexes—it shoots between my legs, cupping my pussy possessively over my gown.

My eyes almost roll back. A low moan escapes as my hips rock into his palm.

"Fuck, baby. That's it. You want it." He presses his fingers against my clit. "With me, you want it."

I nod, breathless. "Uh huh. *Drew.*" Fisting his lapels, I tug his mouth onto mine.

Our kiss turns instantly rough. I rock into his hand like a madwoman, chasing that pleasure . . .

He licks my tongue and moans. "Sex is going to be so good between us, baby. I know you feel it." Tugging my dress out of the way, he dips his hand into the slit. I spread my legs wider, mewling low in my throat. Eyes wild, Drew tugs my tiny, white thong out of the way.

Two fingers slide straight into my soaked cunt, thrusting deep. "Oh God." I'm practically vibrating on this seat, back arching and hips churning. "We shouldn't. We really shouldn't . . ."

"Yes we should, baby. Let yourself feel it." He leans back in to kiss me. That wet tongue and those low, hungry groans drive me crazy. Those fingers fuck me harder, twisting just right. "Come all over my fingers, Lexi."

I do. Sobbing his name, I explode all over his hand, the pleasure shattering every part of me.

It's so good I can't stop rocking my hips, even after I've stopped coming. Drew kisses me as I twitch from the aftershocks. "This is so wrong. We have to stop doing this."

"How is it wrong?" He continues to lazily swirl his soaked fingers inside me.

"I . . . I don't trust you and you haven't given me a reason to . . . to . . ." I choke as those fingers push in deep again.

"What do you need to trust me?"

I'm a hot mess, his hand drenched in my orgasm, but I still manage to focus enough to ask, "Barnard. Andrew, did . . . did you kill him?"

Andrew stares solemnly into my eyes. Fingers still pushed inside me, his palm still pressed to my clit, he calmly says, "Yes, Lexi. Yes I did."

chapter 69

lexi

present

"Lexi. You haven't said anything. Talk to me."

We're on the long line of cars slowly making their way up the winding driveway to the manor. I think I went into shock after Andrew confessed. Numb, I remained silent for the rest of the ride here.

He curses softly under his breath. "Now you're scared of me."

That's the problem. "I'm not." At least not for the reasons I *should* be scared of him.

His surprise is palpable in the interior of the car. "No?"

I shake my head without looking at him. "He was your best friend once." And he killed him.

"You said it. *Was*. We stopped being friends after that entire bullshit went down years ago."

"Why did they stop talking to you? Because you threw them

under the bus?"

Andrew chuckles, but it's a mirthless sound. "*I* stopped talking to *them*. Want nothing to do with those bastards."

My breathing falters. "That never made any sense. You guys all planned it together. Why would you want to stop speaking to them?"

His silence almost tempts me to turn around.

Almost.

"Andrew, I'm warning you. Start making sense. All three of you were thick as thieves growing up. Everyone thought you were all like brothers."

"Lexi, they didn't give a fuck about that. If they had, they would've respected how much you mean to me."

My head turns in his direction all on its own.

He pulls up in front of the valet. "If he cared, he never would've allowed Stephen to get away with hurting you."

There's no time for me to respond. He exits the car and walks around to hand the keys to the valet. I watch him the whole time, blinking back tears.

Dark, evil things have been done to me throughout my life, but never *for* me. No one's ever . . . *cared* that much.

Fuck. Fuck. Fuck. I'm really going to cry.

Drew opens the door.

On trembling legs, I exit the vehicle—and drag him directly to me. His lips meld around mine, in spite of his shock. My blood pounds in my veins, one statement repeating itself in my mind.

For me. He did this for me.

His arms snap around me, crushing me to him. One hand lands possessively on my ass, cupping me in front of everyone.

I don't care. I need him.

His tongue slides into my mouth and I open for it, letting him dominate me. The low groan that vibrates in his chest sets me on fire.

Struggling to catch his breath, he ends our kiss, but leaves his lips against mine. "Tonight, I'm having you, Lexi." He squeezes my ass *hard*. "You know that right?"

I smooth my hands along his wide chest. "First, you're going to explain everything to me."

He shakes his head and kisses me softly. "After."

Only three days into having him back in my life and this man has me so horny that I actually agree to his terms. "Okay." I still don't trust him, still don't know the truth of what happened on his end.

For all I know, he truly did betray me seven years ago. I'll be sleeping with my enemy. *Again.*

Someone clears their throat.

Andrew and I turn as one, his arms still around me.

Asad smiles at us, a happy, pleased smile. As if we're old friends and he's so glad to see us. He's wearing a black tux, his thick black hair slicked back. "Andrew, my friend. I'm afraid I didn't fully understand your meaning earlier."

"You did," Drew replies evenly.

Asad shrugs. "I suspected. I admit, but this is still pleasantly surprising." Holding his hands out, he turns that sincere smile my way. "But I see that she truly is yours. Congratulations are in order, my friend."

There's only one word for this man, this . . . *individual* with his friendly, pleased smile. He's beyond creepy. And beyond insane. That smile may appear pleasant and well-intentioned, but I can't stop the shiver that goes down my spine.

Pulling me away from the car and toward the entrance, Drew pauses long enough to address Asad one final time. "I see you forgot what I told you about not looking at her."

Throwing his head back, Asad laughs. "No. No. But you'd have to be a dead man not to look. You know it's true."

My wide eyes move to Drew.

His lips twitch. Other than that, he evinces no emotion. No

reaction.

Until he speaks again.

"I also warned you not to think about her or even dream about her."

That cold tone . . .

That smile on Asad's face somehow gets even wider. "Now I know you aren't serious. She's a vision. You cannot expect any living man not to think *and* dream about her."

This time, Drew's lips part slowly into his own wide, happy smile. "Thank you for clarifying what the problem is for me. I see what I must do now."

I swear to God, my heart stops beating. My body goes cold. Realization is like a loud, painful slap. That man just called death onto himself and he doesn't even know it.

chapter 70

lexi

present

the echelon of New Jersey society mills about the manor, engrossed in various forms of mutual ass-kissing. Still, most people turn to watch us as we enter, their eyes focusing mostly on Drew.

Morbid curiosity lights up their expressions and suddenly it's obvious—I may have found a way to isolate myself from the tragedy of what happened to Andrew years ago, but these vultures didn't.

No doubt, they ate it up.

They probably followed every headline, dissected every update. Took pleasure at his fall, in that way that only the privileged and bored can.

Now, as we walk past the main foyer, they're all hungry for a piece of him. Maybe some just want his money, his power.

Most of the women, though? It's obvious what they want. An

acrid wave of jealousy bursts free, nearly blinding me.

Andrew's arm tightens around me. At first, I think it's because he sensed my rising aggression, but when I look up at him, I notice that he's glaring at someone.

I turn my head to follow his stare.

A group of men are standing over by one of the bars and most of them are eyeing me. Andrew's fingers flex around my hip before he steers me to the other side of the ballroom. He's practically vibrating with leashed energy. We make it halfway across the ballroom.

All of a sudden, as we're walking by the dance floor, a sea of people ahead of us seems to part in slow motion. On the other side of the divide, a tall, black-haired man comes into view, standing perfectly still.

As if he'd been waiting for us.

The smirk on his face stretches into a full-blown smile.

I almost trip at the sight of him. Andrew tightens his arm around me to steady me, but it's too late.

Years of abuse come barreling back into my awareness. My vision blacks out, skin going cold—

"Stephen, wh-what—oh God, please! Get off!" It's dark, I can't see, but his hands are everywhere. I can't get him off.

"Stay still, Lexi," he pants into my ear.

Revulsion nearly suffocates me.

I kick, flail, scream. He doesn't stop and I know no one will hear me! Not here, in this hidden room, in his massive skyscraper, in the middle of the night.

My panties are ripped off. Teeth chattering from the fear, I start sobbing. "P-please. I've never had sex." Unbidden, Andrew Drevlow's face flashes through my mind and I start crying harder.

Stephen forces himself between my legs, but I keep fighting, nearly hyperventilating. "Let me have what's mine, Lexi!"

The blow to my face stuns me.

By the time I come back to, I feel something hot pressing against my entrance—a single hard thrust and I'm screaming at the top of my lungs as my pussy tears around the invasion—

"Lexi? Lexi!"

That low hiss snaps me back to reality. Blinking, I look around. We're no longer by the dancefloor. We're in a large hallway, backed up inside an alcove.

Drew is in front of me, his hands on my face, worried eyes glittering. "Baby, talk to me."

I whisper his name, chest racing, eyes watering.

Rage clouds his expression, and the switch is so rapid that primal fear slithers through me. It's a deadly calm and detached look. A determined one. "I'm going to kill him. Right the fuck now." He starts to move away.

My hands snap around his wrists, stopping him. "No. *No.* Not like this." A whirlwind of turmoil razes my mind, but I shove it all down. Ignore it. I have to. If the man in front of me sees me break one more time, he's going to murder Stephen.

Here.

In front of all these people.

He won't care. He's past that point.

"Drew, not like this," I repeat, voice somehow steady. Trembling, I lift his hands back to my cheeks; he cups my face again immediately. "There's no coming back from this." *No coming back to me.* I don't dare say that second part aloud.

Maybe he picks up on it anyway. That contained violence in him recedes, replaced once again by his worry. His thumbs caress my cheeks. "It was so bad that you're still having flashbacks from it."

One comment, and the final proof that without me saying the exact words, Andrew knows I was raped.

"Andrew, is that you?"

Drew turns his head to stare over his shoulder.

I remove his hands from my face and peek around him.

Just as he tenses, the danger beginning to rise in him again, I see Stephen Menahan standing there, a pretty blonde on his arm.

A blonde whose baby-doll blue eyes are wide with glee. "It is you! I'm so glad to see you."

Stephen's eyes land on mine, and slowly his lips curl into a self-satisfied smile.

It takes seconds for my brain to jump through a thousand different conclusions, but only one leaves me chilled down to my soul.

A low, rough sound leaves Drew. "Menahan, get your fucking eyes off her. *Now*."

The woman on Stephen's arm jumps at the tone of Andrew's voice.

Stephen ignores Drew's warning, full-on smiling now, that same vicious smile Asad wore earlier—the smile of a monster. "I find this to be a bit embarrassing Drew. Turns out, we may have a bad habit of sharing bed partners."

chapter 71

<u>lexi</u>
present

there's no time for anyone to react. A group of laughing people exit the ballroom and immediately they spot us.

"Menahan! Drevlow!"

For some reason, hearing those two names combined is what tips me over the edge. As the people close in on us, all dying for the attention of both powerful men next to me, I turn around and flee.

Running. Like the coward I am.

I only make it three feet before I bump into a blonde man with light gray eyes.

"Whoa, Lexi! Where you going?" He grabs my arms.

Speechless, I stare up at him, shocked by the sight of him . . . but of course. "You've been with him this whole time."

"Finn, hands. Off. Now."

Finn drops his hands like I'm a hot piece of coal.

Drew comes up behind me, his arm slipping around my waist once more.

And I snap.

"Let go of me!" I hiss.

"United front, Lexi. United front." Ignoring the people calling out his name behind him, he begins walking. Finn falls into step next to me.

Without turning around, I can still feel Stephen's eyes glued to my back the entire time.

"I don't want your hands on me," I growl, teeth grinding.

"We're going to talk about this. But not here. Not now."

That logical tone somehow breaks my heart more.

Yet, it makes sense that he doesn't get it. It doesn't matter to him. And it shouldn't matter to me, but it does.

"Get. The. Fuck. Off. Me. I'll walk on my own."

"You know that's not happening."

The certainty in his voice is enough to merit a kick in the face. Is he fucking kidding me? Forever bossing me around. "In two seconds, whatever your little brilliant plan is, it'll be ruined. You need it to look like I'm on your side." I smile up at him sweetly as we walk by a second group of people. "My fist meeting your face is going to make that a bit difficult to believe, don't you think?" I turn my head away from him once more.

Finn stares at us nervously. "Are you guys having . . . like a couple's argument? 'Cause if so, I can leave."

"No!" I snap.

"Yes," the asshole next to me calmly replies.

A couple's argument? Is he fucking crazy? Scratch that. I *know* he is. However, so am I, and my emotions are spiraling out of control. "Andrew Drevlow."

"Shit," Finn mumbles next to me. "She's full-naming you. Maybe you should—"

A glare from Andrew quickly shuts Finn up.

I try to move away again.

His arm tightens and that stare turns in my direction next. "You aren't going anywhere."

"I already went through this with Stephen."

"Go ahead, baby. Keep fucking comparing me to him."

"How can I not?" I counter, chin raised.

His nostrils flare, eyes blazing. I can't tell if that's anger, lust, or a combination of both.

But, God, that expression—I rip my stare away. *Don't you dare get aroused now.*

Too late. Can't help it when it comes to that bastard.

"You still haven't let me go. I find it hilarious how you haven't done so yet." Grinding my teeth, I try to think of my mom. Of my burning hatred for Stephen. Of why I can't lose control and show the world just how much discord there is between *my boss* and I.

There's no need to analyze why I'm so furious now. And, yes, it's petty of me, possibly childish, but I can't help but be hurt.

I mean, come on. It's not like I could've expected that he'd have waited for me seven years. Why the hell does the knowledge that he slept with Stephen's current toy break my heart?

Maybe because I spent the last several years being abused over and over, and Andrew was clearly out there still enjoying himself.

I can't begrudge him that, but the fury and possessiveness I feel continues to choke me. Doesn't matter what I tell myself.

"Mr. Drevlow!"

Andrew doesn't slow down one bit.

Finn stares over his shoulder, then curses. "Stop. That's Mr. Holtzman himself."

Cursing under his breath, Drew listens, and I'm shocked when he turns us back around to wait for the middle-aged man heading our way. "I have to speak with him. No choice."

Another part of the plan I wasn't aware of.

Hold on. My back straightens and it takes all my willpower to hide my surprise. *I've only been back three days.* But Andrew's plan is too detailed to have been planned in that short span of time. I turn my head and find him staring at me. Just how long has he been putting all this together?

"Mateo, please, stay with Lexi," is all Andrew says before letting me go.

I look over my shoulder, seeing my bodyguard standing behind us. Where the hell did he come from?

"Finn," Drew says. They both walk toward Mr. Holtzman, meeting him halfway.

I spin around, grateful. Need solitude. Mateo is quick on my heels as I head down the hall, but that's fine.

I have a way to lose him.

"Ms. Berkman, where are you—"

"This way." A right turn puts us in front of yet another entrance back to the ballroom.

chapter 72

lexi

present

a t the very end of it, I see the grand staircase leading up to the second floor.

I lead us through the ballroom with single-minded focus, uncaring if people notice. Mateo follows me halfway up the stairs before speaking again. "Ms. Berkman, why are we heading to the second floor?"

Because I'm hoping to find some privacy to get rid of you. "I'm sure there's a more private bathroom away from the main party." I slip my hand into my royal blue clutch, feeling around for the small pocket injector. Paul gave it to me months ago for protection. It looks like an insulin pen, but it's really a tranquilizer.

Yes. I know. Fucked up. Extreme. But I have the dosage set to only deliver a small amount. Considering Mateo's size, I doubt he'll be out for long.

I just need to get away so I can have some privacy while I cry these ridiculous emotions out. My bodyguard isn't going to give me any privacy. His boss wouldn't allow it.

Guess it makes sense why I'm willing to take such drastic measures to get what I want. When dealing with men that have enough power to limit your choice, you become just as callous as them to get your way.

Mateo starts speaking behind me. I don't pay attention, just speed up my movements, rushing us down a large hallway. He's gaining on me, can feel it, is probably a second away from grabbing my arm to halt me.

The gigantic hallway is empty, and nothing but statues and hung paintings seem to be around.

Mateo grabs my arm.

In a split second, I swing around and jam the tiny needle into his neck.

The drug doesn't hit right away, the dose is too low, but as his eyes widen, I see the haze start to cloud them.

If I stay even a second longer, he'll be able to grab and restrain me until he fully passes out.

So I bolt.

I hear him call out my name, but ignore it, turning sharply. Down another hallway and yet another turn.

By now he must have passed out.

Panting, I slow to a stop and begin checking door after door. They're all locked, which actually surprises me although it shouldn't.

Of course most of the rooms would be closed off to guests. The Holtzman family actually *lives* here. I release the knob on the last door I tried and step back.

A woman in a server's uniform steps out of another room. She startles when she sees me. "Miss?"

Fuck.

Schooling my expression, I turn fully. "Just looking for the restroom."

She smiles at me. "The ones downstairs are that packed already?"

I nod, smiling back.

"Here." She steps aside and holds open the door she just exited from. "This is a bathroom."

This time, the smile I give her is genuine and full of gratitude, I'm sure. I rush past her, heart racing, wondering where Mateo passed out and if she'll walk in that direction and stumble upon him.

She lets the door close behind her. I hurry over to the counter and drop my clutch on it, uncaring that all the contents spill out into the sink. Squeezing the edge of the counter, I stare into the mirror.

Is it just me or do my gray eyes seem freakier than usual?

Of course they do. I've gone certifiably crazy. Jesus Christ, did I really drug my two-hundred-something-pound bodyguard just to get away from him and have a moment to myself?

"Who are you?" I can't help but whisper at the frantic girl in the mirror.

Fuck, I'm so heartbroken. Irrational. I haven't been normal for a long time now, I know this, but this is different. It's like Andrew's fist is inside my chest, squeezing my heart, commanding it to react to *everything* about him.

I can't hate him for finding pleasure outside of me. Just because I couldn't move on from him, because Stephen abused me and also took that from me, doesn't mean I get to hate Drew for living his life.

So why does it feel like I do?

I cover my face with my hands, trying to bring my hair-trigger emotions back under control.

The knob turns.

Crap. I forgot to lock it.

"A moment please!" I call, spinning to grab the door before it opens—

It does, and the tall figure that fills the doorway makes me freeze.

Smiling that pleased, good-natured smile of his, Asad steps inside. "There you are, beautiful girl. I couldn't believe my luck when I saw you drug your bodyguard."

That look in his eyes.

That smile.

I know all of it. Saw that intent in the eyes of another man one too many times to mistake it.

Stepping back, I growl at him. "Stay the fuck away from me."

Without looking behind him, he closes the door. "Lexi, is it? This will go much easier for you if you just let yourself enjoy it. I promise you, I am a giving lover. If you don't fight me, I can make it feel amazing for you."

chapter 73

andrew

7 years ago

"*When are you going to stop drugging my son?*"

That voice reaches me from far away, barely recognizable in my mind.

"*Your son? You mean mine.*"

The sound of my violently pounding heart fills my head. *Rage*. The emotion is so strong that I can almost hear it speaking to me.

"*Ronald, it's been two weeks!*"

It's those words that finally bring consciousness roaring to the full front.

Two weeks.

Two-fucking-weeks?

My eyes fly open. It takes a while for my vision to focus enough for me to make out details.

What the fuck did that asshole drug me with?

The walls of my room come into view. That isn't what catches my attention. No. The two, huge men standing just inside the double-doors of my room are.

Greg. Dominic. Two of my dad's main bodyguards. They weren't there that day on the porch . . .

That day *two weeks* ago.

She's been gone that long.

I'll never find her.

Everything I am revolts at that idea.

I open my mouth but my throat is so dry I can't form any words. Dominic glances over, black eyes widening as he realizes I'm awake. He taps Greg on the shoulder before heading over to the nightstand, where a pitcher of water and a glass are.

When he approaches me with the half-full glass, I have no choice but to accept it. My throat is too dehydrated. Speaking will be impossible like this.

Lexi has a two-week head start. She can be anywhere in the world by now. Especially with the nice sum of money I'm sure my father gave her.

I know he's responsible for this.

Fuming, I chug the water down.

Greg opens the door and leans out.

My parents are out there. That's what I heard.

Immediately, I hand the glass over to Dominic. With a speed I shouldn't possess, I throw my legs over the side of the bed.

My mother rushes in first, tears in her eyes.

Love her to death but I'm not focused on her. No. The smug piece of shit stepping into my room is the one I need to get at.

Mom tries to throw her arms around me. I hold up a hand to stop her, eyes on Ronald Drevlow, the bag of garbage that sired me. "Where did you help them move to?"

He simply shakes his head and turns to Greg. "As I predicted. His first thought upon waking up is her." Turning to lean out the door, he calls out, "Roderick! Miles!"

I recognize those two names.

Pretty sure those were two of the assholes that helped my father drug me.

To my still somewhat sluggish senses, everything around me seems to happen in slow motion.

"Get her out of here," Ronald orders Dominic.

My head wipes around in time to see Dominic lifting my much smaller Mom off her feet. Mom kicks and screams, as he all but flies out the room with her.

Roaring, I shoot off the bed, legs unsteady.

Roderick, Greg, and Miles come at me, surrounding me, their strength unsurpassable. Especially with that fucking drug still pumping through my body. As one, they lift me off my feet and throw me on the bed.

I try to lunge off but I'm not quick enough.

"Fuck you, you bastard!" I yell at my father, struggling against them all. "You did this! You're the reason she's gone!"

"Drew!" My mother screeches from the hallway.

"I'll kill you!" Thrashing in the bodyguards' hold, I watch as Ronald approaches a table by the door. On it, is an entire case full of more syringes.

He plucks one, a cold smile on his face.

"I'll kill you! I SWEAR ON EVERYTHING I AM, I WILL KILL YOU!" My voice breaks with the force of my roar. "I'll kill you all!"

"Ronald, leave my son alone!" My mother's wail can barely be heard above my shouts.

"Now, now. Evelyn, calm down, before I have to do this to you as well." Ronald approaches the left side of my bed, where all three of his pathetic puppets are bearing down on me with all their weight.

"Don't you fucking touch her!" I'm so far gone that spit flies out of my mouth.

Ronald's lip curls up into a sneer. "Look at you. Like a rabid animal over that girl. That's why I'm going to continue drugging you until you get it through your head that it's over, boy."

I'm still vowing the vengeance on them when the man I hate the most in the world—the man half responsible for me existing in it—leans down and jabs the needle back into my neck.

chapter 74

lexi
present

i've taken self-defense classes in the last few years.

In my room, watching videos, but the grueling practice I engaged in was real.

So many hours preparing for this. And all the moves, all the openings, all the shots I can take, rush through my mind at top speed.

Logically, I know I can fight back. That I have the *skill* to do so.

But, emotionally, it takes me a few seconds too long.

Asad reaches for me.

Finally—*finally*—I burst into action, screaming at the top of my lungs. I lift my knee to catch him wherever I can, but Asad throws his entire weight into me, slamming my back into the marble counter behind me.

I cry out from the pain, arms wailing.

My elbow connects with the side of his face.

A monstrous sound leaves him. Pain explodes through my scalp as he pulls my hair and whirls me around.

I'm still fighting, kicking, screaming, unlike with Stephen. I won't check out like I did with—

Click.

The barrel of a gun presses into the back of my head.

All the fight leaves me. *Instantly.* Eyes wide, I stare at the reflection in the mirror, confirming what I felt.

Asad smiles at me in the reflection, pressing the gun against my head harder. "There now. One hit, I'll let you get away with"—he runs the fingers of his free hand down my back, toward the curve of my ass—"because you are so, so exquisite." The same hand he just caressed me with drops down to just below my ass, fisting my skirt. "I must have you, and I prefer not to have to kill you while at it."

Fight back. Doesn't matter. It's better to die than to let another man rape you. I tell myself that over and over, but the truth is that Andrew's face is once again at the forefront of my mind.

And the thought of leaving this Earth now that we're together again . . .

"He'll kill you," I whisper, tears sliding down my cheeks.

Asad laughs, shoving my skirt up my ass. "I'll kill him before he gets to me, so let's agree to a mutual fucking."

"Fuck you, you sick bastard. There's nothing mutual about this."

"There can be."

My thong drops to my ankles.

My eyes dart to the injector inside the sink. If only I could . . . Not with this gun to my head.

The sound of Asad's belt buckle pings through the bathroom. I close my eyes, cold metal against my head reminding me why I can't fight.

Then again, what's to stop him from killing me after?

Stupid. Stupid. Stupid. If I hadn't drugged Mateo, he'd be here. This wouldn't be happening to me. "You don't understand. Andrew *will*—"

I'm slammed forward, face pressed against the mirror. At my back, Asad lays over me, growling, "Don't you dare say his name again until I'm done."

The familiar sensation of being penetrated with no lubrication slams through me. I gasp, choking. He's inside me. It's hurting. God, it's—

The door flies open, hitting Asad.

In the blink of an eye, he's off me, and an unholy snarl rents the air.

Legs failing me, I spin around, almost lifting myself onto the counter from the fear.

Asad is thrown into the far left wall.

The door is thrown closed next.

A mad blur flies toward my rapist. A fist connects with his face.

By the time I recognize it's Andrew, he has Asad on the floor, his hands wrapped around his neck.

And he's squeezing. He's squeezing down so hard that Asad's tanned face is already turning blue.

Stop him, my mind screams, but I'm frozen. He's doing it. He's killing a man for harming me, and he's doing it right in front of me.

Asad struggles to get his thumb into Andrew's eye-socket.

In a rage at the thought of Drew's eye being hurt, I finally push away from the counter. Within seconds, I'm on the floor, fighting to get my hands around Asad's wrists. His dark eyes bulge at the realization that I'm grabbing him.

I'm holding his hands down.

I'm helping Drew kill him.

"Lexi, move away!" Drew growls, eyes flickering toward me.

Holding Asad's wrists to the floor, I look into those toffee-colored, dilated eyes. "No." The only way for me to release this piece of shit is if Andrew releases him.

If he lets him live, I let him live.

But if Drew is going to end him for me, murder yet another man in my name . . .

This time, I'm going to help him. I've never killed a man before, but Drew isn't doing this for me on his own.

Asad's choked gasps taper off. Drew's still looking into my eyes; I'm still looking into his. Neither one of us look away as the man below us loses consciousness.

We continue looking into each other's eyes long after Asad's heart stops beating.

"You should've let him go, Lexi." Andrew's panting, eyes tormented.

"You should have, too," I whisper.

He jerks his head. "*He was inside you.*"

"And you killed him for it," my voice hushes out.

"He . . . was . . . fucking . . . *inside* you!"

"You saved me." I let Asad's wrists go, following Drew as he shoots to his feet. "This time around, *you* saved me."

REVIEW TEAM

Want to join my official review/hype team and get free reader copies, goodies, and more?

Come on over, then!

Click here to sign up: https://bit.ly/nibelites2

ABOUT THE AUTHOR

N. Isabelle Blanco is the *Amazon Bestselling Author* of the Allure Series, the Need Series with K.I.Lynn, and many others. At the age of three, due to an odd fascination with studying her mother's handwriting, she began to read and write. By the time she'd reached kindergarten, she had an extensive vocabulary and her obsession with words began to bleed into every aspect of her life.

That is, until coffee came a long and took over everything else.

Nowadays, N. spends most of her days surviving the crazy New York rush and arguing with her characters every ten minutes or so, all in the hopes of one day getting them under control.

Sign up for the newsletter at https://bit.ly/NIBsignup to be the first to know how all these arguments turn out :)

ALSO BY N. ISABELLE BLANCO

Ryze Series
(Dark Paranormal Romance)
Lust
Silence
Vengeance
Cursed
Hunt
Sacrifice
Light (Coming Soon)

Allure Series
(Contemporary Romance)
To Want You
To Have You
To Lose You

Retaliations Series
(Romantic Suspense)
A Debt Repaid
Damage Owed (Coming Soon)

Siege Series
(Dark Romantic Suspense)
Twisted Heartbreak
Twisted Rage

Need Series (Co-written w/ K.I. Lynn)
(New Adult Angst)
Need
Take
Own

Want exclusive teasers to all my upcoming work?
Join my Facebook reader group: Haus of N.